Roch & Mo...
To you both — you...
life-livers!
with love & thanks,
Helen May
2016

MOTHER TONGUE

by Helen May

Illustrations by Marc Luc Poelvoorde

◆ FriesenPress

Suite 300 - 990 Fort St
Victoria, BC, Canada, V8V 3K2
www.friesenpress.com

Illustrator: Marc Luc Poelvoorde

ISBN
978-1-4602-8342-4 (Paperback)
978-1-4602-8343-1 (eBook)

1. Fiction, Contemporary Women

Distributed to the trade by The Ingram Book Company

Dedication

To Rolf. Your unstinting generosity has made this book a reality. Thank you, dear friend.

Preface

When I was a little girl, even before learning to read I had the notion that every story in the world hovered like a drop of dew on the lip of a leaf at daybreak. The instant a storyteller begins to speak a story the dewdrop plummets to the sun-warmed earth where it transforms into bountiful drops imbued with characters, situations, relationships, and most often, a transformation of some kind. Throughout my long life, plummeting drops of dew, if you will, have been ever-present.

I grew up hearing stories told in the language of the Zulu people, a lyrical language rich in descriptive metaphors. Their manner of inclusion is expressed, for example, by the use of "we," "us," and "ours," rather than "I," "me," and "mine." They had a story for every occasion: teaching stories, tales to dry tears, legends to broaden a child's mind, and comical and compassionate stories. Stories were honed in the oral tradition that provided a foundation for my evolution into a storyteller.

After many years of living and telling stories onstage in Canada, I was motivated to take my oral storytelling from the stage to the page. My speaking voice, body language, and gestures told the story onstage. The audience fuelled inspiration and provided encouragement. I was challenged to find my writing voice, though, to reach into the depths of my interior life for inspiration, to find solace in solitude while setting my imagination free to find the words.

It is my hope that you, dear reader, will hear my voice speaking to you on these pages since most of the stories in this collection have made the transition from stage to page.

The first story, "Eggs Explained," introduces Madelaine at age four in 1943. She lives in a spacious farmhouse situated on hundreds of acres in South Africa. Her mother, a remote and unwell woman, leaves her in the care of Zulu staff. They speak her mother tongue and their loving kindness leaves an indelible imprint on her sense of self.

Impending laws of racial segregation are about to go into effect in South Africa. That, intertwined with Madelaine's discovery that she is not a Zulu, shatters her sense of belonging. For decades, Madelaine searches for this lost sense of belonging. As the daughter of a privileged, colonial, English-speaking family whose embrace she does not feel welcomed by, and being too young to cope with her biological family's expectations to adhere to rules that govern colonial daughters, Madelaine develops a patience of sorts, and an undaunted spirit.

We follow Madelaine and her husband's flight from the politics of South Africa, encouraged by Nelson Mandela. Their journey takes them by ship to Rio de Janeiro. Within three years, political instability in Brazil compels them to find a home elsewhere. They embark on an unbelievable road trip, driving from Rio de Janeiro to Vancouver, Canada.

No matter how deeply engaged and contented Madelaine is as the mother of two sons, she realizes that her husband no longer loves her. A yearning for her roots, to speak in her mother tongue, and in fact the need to settle a soul debt with the tribal people of

South Africa, reaches a pitch she has to act upon. In "Crane's Call," she faces this driving need and takes steps towards fulfilling it.

The final story—"The Court"—takes place in 2005. Madelaine is provided with an opportunity she cannot ignore. Were it not for Madelaine's mother tongue, she would very likely not have recognized the humanizing effect of forgiveness.

Acknowledgements

Davina Haisell. My treasured editor. Your patience and thought-provoking mark-ups, the respect with which you work on my trials, saying it like it is, have moved these stories from stage to page. Your editorial work is remarkable and thorough, and I'm so fortunate to have worked with you.

Conlan Mansfield. I thank you for sharing your bright, incisive mind with me, and for your keen ability to listen to my reading and offer the astute suggestions that encouraged me towards the path of vernacular eloquence, as written about by Peter Elbow in his book of the same name.

Pauline Wenn and Dunc Shields. Thank you for launching me into the world of storytelling in Vancouver, and for your warm-hearted support. You both offered "a string for my kite" by showing me ways to catch the essence of story.

My dear friends. You know who you are. Thank you for listening to my stories over decades of camaraderie, for reading my initial attempts at writing, and for pointing out my tendency (now past, I hope) to mute my passion on the page.

Gratitude for my loved family is limitless. You all energize me with reasons to live purposefully and with meaning, to remain strong, flexible, and secure in the knowledge we share.

I acknowledge the Indigenous people of this world with respect. Thank you for taking me into your midst with unquestioned trust and kindness.

Contents

EGGS EXPLAINED

Madelaine's home, built of mud and stone in the 1800s, sits on the side of a hill overlooking a wide valley with a river flowing through it. A farmhouse with many rooms, it has deep verandas that cool the air coming in through the open doors and windows. In this part of South Africa summer days are bright with sunshine, but when the afternoon breezes die down the heat is intense. Late on most afternoons a thunderstorm comes crashing through, lightning hisses and crackles, a cool wind blows through the house, and heavy rain hammers on the tin roof. After the storm moves on, sunshine returns to a rain-washed and sparkling world that never fails to lift Madelaine's young heart.

One hot afternoon, the whole world seems to be napping. Flowers in the gardens have droopy heads and the birds are not singing. Four-year-old Madelaine is lonely for someone to talk to.

She wanders around the living room looking for something to do, eventually sitting in each of the armchairs like Goldilocks, whispering, "And this chair is Father's, this chair is Mother's …".

Framed photographs on the mantle above the fireplace catch her eye, and one in particular. But, the mantle is much too high to reach, so she drags a side table over, climbs onto it, and puts her face close to the black-and-white photograph to examine it. Her older sister had told her it is of Madelaine and her mother in 1940, at her christening eight weeks after she was born. This felt so important that she clearly remembers her sister's words.

Madelaine's mother is wearing beautiful high heels. Her head is turned to look at the baby held in the crook of her arm, and she is smiling. The child is dressed in a christening gown that flows down from below her chin to the hem of her mother's coat, which reaches to her calves. Madelaine's face is a small blur under a lace cap.

While standing on the table, engrossed in the photograph, she sees her reflection in the framed glass. Wild curls spring from her head. Some twisted into dreadlocks by Zilli hang down by her ears. Madelaine looks into the eyes of her reflection, then down at her knobby knees and dusty, broad bare feet. She takes another look at the baby covered in white and tries to find its knees under the copious material that looks like a waterfall. She can't find the baby's knees, so she puts the picture back, climbs down from the table, and drags it back into place.

Madelaine wonders if the afternoon is over and if her friends have returned from their break. The door to the kitchen is closed, but the smells of mopped stone floors and wood smoke make her think they could be back. She hopes they feel like talking; a story would be even better.

Bazo's shoes are sitting at the side of the kitchen door. He walks to work from his house down by the river and always leaves his shoes in that spot. Bazo is in charge of everything in the kitchen and the pantry. He knows how to drive a tractor, plant a garden, polish shoes, mend horse halters, and is a wonderful cook.

Zilli's shoes are there beside his. She takes care of Madelaine, shows her how to do things for herself, and, like Bazo, is good at doing many things: laundry, ironing, sewing, mending, polishing the silver, and of course, looking after Madelaine.

Zilli lives not too far away—close enough for Madelaine to visit her and her family, especially Figele, her daughter. Figele is Madelaine's age, and her friend. Zilli has three houses: one where she, the girls, and babies sleep, one where her husband and the boys sleep, and one where the family eats. The houses are round and have thatched roofs and mud walls painted with red, white, blue, and green designs.

Madelaine knows the eating house because that is where the family shares their food with her. They sit on grass mats around a big black pot of stew that is heating over the fire. Next to that pot is a smaller one containing *putu*: stiff cornmeal porridge. The children are each given a wooden bowl full of stew. They use their hands to shape the *putu* like a sausage, which they dip into and scoop the stew with. The smell of wood smoke and food—and that special scent of Zilli's body, just like a warm stone by the river—makes Madelaine want to live with Zilli and her family.

Bazo is good at many things, especially explaining things to Madelaine. One time, she found her brother's collection of birds' eggs. Each egg was sitting in its own bed of soft wool, and they were all lined up on a special tray. Madelaine thought she could set the flock free by sitting on the eggs to hatch them. Very carefully, she sat down on them, just as she had seen hens do in their nests. Then, she heard and felt the eggshells crack and crush under her. Not wanting to believe what was happening, she spread her knees and peered between them at the "nest" she was sitting on. It was true. All the eggs were broken. She jumped up and ran in search of Bazo, whom she found in the pantry.

"You have to come now! Now, to help me!"

Clutching Bazo's hand on the way back to her brother's room, she tells him about her plan to hatch the eggs and free the birds inside. He listens, but doesn't say anything.

They stop at the tray of crushed eggs. He holds his chin in his hand, clears his throat, and makes a deep rumbling sound. "Hmmm? Uh-hmmm."

Bazo nods his head, takes Madelaine's hand, and leads her back to the kitchen. He picks her up and sits her on the table so they can see into each other's eyes.

"Now, *nTombi Yethu*,[1] this I must say to you in a way that we two will always remember. It is like this: We don't always know how to do something the right way, and so when we do something that is not the right way, we name this a 'mistake.' When we do a mistake with something that does not belong to us, we must go to the person to whom the thing belongs and tell them about our mistake. Do you feel the knowing of my saying, *nTombi Yethu*?"

Madelaine, listening carefully, nods. Bazo asks if she has a way of doing this—to go to her brother and tell him about the mistake. She nods again, thinking she could tell her brother about the eggs when he comes home from boarding school for the holidays, that it does not have to be today. But Bazo is not finished.

"This thing of the broken eggs," he explains, "it is telling us you have learned that a chicken makes only chickens—that each bird makes its own kind, pumpkins make pumpkins, humans make humans. We do not lay eggs, so that is why humans do not sit on eggs."

One thing Bazo could not explain, however, was why Madelaine's mother was lying in a bed in a room with the door closed, and why the nurse who looked after Madelaine's mother would not allow her into that room to visit.

1   our girl (isiZulu)

Eventually, things begin to change in Madelaine's home. One day she watches a ship dock at the seaside town while sitting on her dad's shoulders, and is told that it is a troop ship bringing home soldiers and nurses who had not been killed in the war. After that day, she is closer to understanding why her uncles and some aunts have been away.

Then, the nurse who was looking after Madelaine's mother left—*forever*, Madelaine hoped. Almost at the same time, her father came home for good, and Madelaine's mother got out of bed.

Having her father home makes Madelaine feel safe. She loves him; she likes the smell of him, the arms that pick her up and hold her close to his chest, the blue of his eyes as he looks directly into hers, and the way he listens when she speaks to him. It feels good to call him "Dad" and to hear his warm voice saying, "My *Tombi*,"[2] which is not that different from the name Zilli and Bazo gave to her: *nTombi Yethu*. Her father speaks to her in the language she knows—isiZulu, the same as Zilli and Bazo's language.

Dad makes her mother happy too, and they keep each other company at the dining room table. He always sits at the head of the table and her mother to his side. They hold hands across the corner of the table when they have finished eating. That is when her mother's eyes sparkle and Madelaine hears her laugh.

Madelaine's sister is thirteen and her brother is ten. They also eat in the dining room, whereas Madelaine eats at a different time and in the kitchen with Bazo and Zilli.

During mealtimes, Madelaine can hear her sister and brother talking (always in English), and if Madelaine tries to join them at the table after her meal, they ignore her. Nothing Madelaine does interests them, it seems.

2 girl (isiZulu)

Her brother paid attention to her for a little while, after she confessed her mistake with his egg collection. He punished her many times—a punishment for each egg she had broken. One punishment was to push her out of his tree fort. She will never follow him up there again, because she fell a long way down onto the hard earth, which made her feel dizzy and sick. He also made her step barefoot into a fresh cowpat and stand there as the squishy stuff oozed through her toes, while he counted to ten very slowly; those sorts of punishments.

Madelaine wants to play with her big sister, but is told to leave her alone and to stop following her around. So, she stops trying to be friends with her sister, who boasts about the rules she knows—rules for girls that Madelaine could not possibly understand until she is old enough to go to school.

Madelaine wonders what she will do at the school in the village, aside from learning rules for girls. Zilli and Bazo have not been to any kind of school. They say it will be good because Madelaine will learn things and make friends with children her age.

"Zilli, your girl Figele is my friend, and Bazo, your boys, nDugu and Qala, they are my friends too. That's enough, isn't it?"

Zilli, Bazo, and Madelaine are on the kitchen veranda having this conversation about friends. Zilli is drying Madelaine's hair and trying to untangle the dreadlocks that have grown past her shoulders. Dad is going to cut her hair for school.

"*nTombi Yethu,*" says Zilli, "friends here at home and also at school is a good thing for anybody, but more so for a special girl like you."

I am special?

Dad comes out to the veranda at this moment, greets each of them, and then wraps a towel around Madelaine's shoulders. Having no mirror, she follows the sound of the scissors from one chop of a bundle of dreadlocks to the next. All four are suddenly gone. Dad combs what hair remains on her head, and snips here and there. Madelaine eyes the ropes of hair lying on the tiles of the veranda like slain snakes then raises her hands to her head and finds nothing is in its usual place. She looks up at Dad to see him watching her face.

He will be proud of me.

Determined, instead of crying out, she touches her head carefully with her fingertips, and thankfully, feels hair there. Later, in the bathroom mirror, she tries to match short hair to her face by grinning. That is not much good because she has no teeth. She had knocked out her baby teeth by crashing into the faucets face-first while pretending to be a porpoise in the bathtub. She tries smiling with closed lips, and supposes that looks better somehow. And her head? Her neck—with no locks covering the part under her ears—is bare. Her ears look bigger than they really are. Madelaine not only looks different, but she feels different, and hopes her face will know what to do.

A SPECIAL PLACE

She is to ride to school on Punch, a pony her brother has outgrown. Zondi, who will ride one of her dad's horses, is to accompany her on the five miles that stretch from the farm to the village school, and back home after school. Zondi is Bazo's uncle, and like Bazo he is not very tall, but is strong and gentle. He has crinkly lines around his dark brown eyes, and scars in a pattern across his cheeks, which were made when he was young—scars like Bazo's. Zilli has scars on her cheeks, too. They are in a different pattern because her tribal family is not the same as Zondi's and Bazo's.

Zondi wears jodhpurs, riding boots, and a green shirt. For school, Madelaine wears jodhpurs and riding boots too, and a white shirt. The leather satchel that fits on her back carries her lunch, exercise books, and pencils.

Madelaine is excited and scared; excited about the adventure of going to school, scared about not knowing what to do and where to go when she gets there. Riding in the early morning is one of the things she loves to do. This morning, though, the satchel on her back reminds her that it is a different sort of day.

Madeline and Punch follow Zondi on his horse from the stable yard, down the long driveway between jacaranda trees, across the river, and into the plantations. They don't talk much. She listens to the comforting sound of hoof beats and the clinking sound of the bridle bits, remembering to sit properly in her saddle and hold the reins gently in both hands in front of the saddle. She forgets about being scared.

The main road into the village forks soon after they leave the plantations, and they take the smaller road towards a stand of eucalyptus trees.

Zondi points. "That is your school, *nTombi Yethu.*"

Madelaine sees, amongst the trees, a smallish building made of shiny new sheets of iron. The front door is open. A woman wearing a red dress is standing in the doorway. Boys are running around, chasing each other in-between the trees.

Madelaine and Zondi stop a short distance from the school. He dismounts and tells her to do the same. She hands Punch's reins to him, and listens.

"After your lunch, I will be here to take you home," he says. "*Sala gahle,*[3] *nTombi Yethu.*"

Madelaine does not want to be left here. A crying rises in her chest. That scared feeling returns, stiffens her legs and arms, and makes her ears buzz. She swallows hard to stop the cry from escaping, and looks up at Zondi who is standing between the two horses, their reins in his hands. Still holding the reins, he places his hands on Madelaine's shoulders, looks her in the eyes, and tells her that he cannot take her home right now because that would be breaking an important rule—a rule about young people going to

3   stay well (isiZulu)

school. Warmth and kindness coming through his hands and from his eyes soothe and steady her.

"Stay calm in your heart and you will be strong," he whispers, and then mounts his horse. Leading Punch, he rides away.

Standing on the edge of the road, Madelaine watches the two horses and Zondi until they disappear onto the plantations. Fear is now mixed with love for her companions who have gone from her. She needs to pee, but doesn't know where to go, or even if girls are allowed to pee during school.

The woman wearing the red dress shouts from the doorway and beckons to her. Madelaine walks over, stands in front of her, and greets her. She is about to ask if she can go pee when the woman says something in the language Madelaine's parents speak to each other—English. She tries to concentrate, but this woman's angry voice comes out of a red lipstick mouth. It is hard for Madelaine to understand the words she shouts over and over, and then suddenly Madelaine understands.

"I am your teacher, and you will not speak to me in that *kaffir*[4] tongue. Do you hear me? Now, greet me in English and remember my name: Miss Barrie."

"Good morning, Miss Barrie," Madelaine lisps and says quickly, before she forgets how, "The bathroom, please."

Miss Barrie jabs a finger in the direction of two corrugated iron privies, which were far from the school building.

With a hurried thank you, Madelaine runs to the nearest privy, pulls the door open, and is hit by a terrible smell. In the dark, box-like enclosure she unbuttons her jodhpurs, shuts the door, sits down over a hole in the wooden seat, and relieves herself.

---

4   *kaffir* — a derogatory label for a person of colour.

A bell is ringing. Madelaine steps outside and looks towards the sound. Pupils are lining up to face Miss Barrie, who is standing in the doorway.

Madelaine ends up being the last in line, which makes it easy to follow the others. They seem to know what to do and where to go, but then she has to sit in the last available desk—the one right in front, facing Miss Barrie's desk. After sitting down and putting away school things, each pupil places their hands on top of their desk, palms down. Miss Barrie, holding a metal-edged ruler, goes to each pupil and inspects their hands to see how clean they are. When satisfied that a pupil's hands are clean, she moves to the next pupil. Miss Barrie stops at Madelaine's desk and bends to get a closer look. She straightens up, clamps a hand around Madelaine's wrist, lifts the ruler above her head and brings its metal edge whizzing down. It lands with a stinging *thwack* across Madelaine's knuckles.

Madelaine looks at her hand, a red welt blooming before her eyes. Before she can breathe, Miss Barrie has Madelaine's other wrist clamped in a vice-like grip. Once again, the ruler comes whizzing down. Miss Barrie mutters under her breath while Madelaine struggles to understand: " ... expect ... riding to school with a black ... horse dirt hands ..."

Madelaine is sent to wash her hands in a basin that sits on a metal stand in a corner of the classroom. The water is cold, which soothes her stinging knuckles, but without soap she can't get her hands clean. Anyway, they don't look dirty to her. While scrubbing her knuckles and telling herself not to cry, one of the words Miss Barrie had said comes back to her: "horse dirt." *What is wrong with horse dirt?*

On the way back to her desk she looks at the other pupils instead of at the floor. Although she is accustomed to her brother's teasing ways of making her look stupid, this is not the same. Never has she been looked at by more than one person in that "You are stupid, ha-ha" way before—especially by people she doesn't know. Some faces are pulled into a pretend crybaby look. Others have stuck their tongues out at her. Many are sniggering and whispering behind their hands. A burning, prickly feeling crawls over her body. She wants very much to run out of there and never come back, but Zondi's words, "Stay calm in your heart and you will be strong," nudge her back to her desk. Madelaine is proud of herself for not crying.

For the next while, every day begins this way. Madelaine gets better at knowing what will happen, but she still doesn't know who to talk to about the daily knuckle whipping. She remembers the names of the other pupils: Klingermann, Hauptschloss, van der Merwe. And then one day, on her way to the shady trees to have lunch, she notices something that immediately makes her want to talk to an adult. She will have to wait until it is time to go home.

There are no girls in the school. The school has ten pupils, nine of them boys. Madelaine is the only girl. *Oh.* That means that the rules for girls her big sister boasted about only apply to her.

Madelaine supposes that Miss Barrie is a girl, but she does not count as one—not after what she does to Madelaine's knuckles every morning. Zilli is a girl, a most special kind of grown-up girl.

Madelaine's heart sings when she sees Zondi waiting at the roadside after Miss Barrie has stopped clanging the school bell. She has so much to tell Zondi that she begins talking even while she says "hello" to Punch, and is still chattering while she mounts and pulls away from the school as quickly as she can. Soon, Madelaine and Zondi are on the path through the plantations.

"Zondi, tell me what *kaffir* means, please."

Zondi reins in his horse and waits for Madelaine to come abreast. He runs a hand over his head, shaking it solemnly from side to side. "Tell me, *nTombi Yethu*, who used that word?"

After she tells him, his expression changes into one that Madelaine has not seen before. There is sadness and a faraway look in his eyes. He takes a deep breath and sighs. He will ask her dad about this. When she asks what she can do about being hit on the knuckles, if that is a rule for girls she should know about, and if he could explain it to her, he gets upset; so much so, he chivies his horse to a canter. Madelaine nudges Punch with her heels to keep up with him. Cantering feels good, as does the air on her face and getting far away from the tin shack where Miss Barrie shouts and the boys pull faces at her.

It's really hard to feel calm in her heart when she is at school, especially when Miss Barrie hits her on the knuckles; when the boys call her names like "*kaffir* lover" and "miss no-teeth"; and when she has to kick and fight the boys off while they grab at her and try to get her knickers off (which they can't, because luckily there's too many buttons on her jodhpurs for them to rip off).

Madelaine loves to read. Her counting is pretty good. Writing with a pen that must be dipped in the inkpot on her desk is tough because her hand shakes after being hit with the ruler. She makes a mess with ink on the pages of the book. Madelaine remembers to speak English, but the other language—Afrikaans—will just not go into her head. Everyone else knows that language well. Some of the older boys also speak German.

One morning, Madelaine awakes feeling fed up with trying to be good about going to school. Her stomach hurts. Her teeth will not hurry up and grow. She has no friends. Miss Barrie does not like her. She has had enough of being hit with a ruler, and is tired of being chased, grabbed at, and called bad names by the boys.

Dad and Mum are at the dining table eating breakfast. Madelaine knows she is not allowed to disturb them, but there are too many questions she wants to ask.

Zondi has tried to help her understand, but lately he just says, "This, *nTombi Yethu*, must be talked with your father about."

She remembers the rule about learning Zondi had told her during one of their rides home after school: "There is no sense in fighting against what we know we must learn. We begin by learning to survive, and then we do better and begin to learn how to live. So, there are rules we learn, and know how to follow. But, *nTombi Yethu*, there is no sense in following the path of fear or hatred. That is a rule you must lay down for yourself, and do not break it ..."

Madelaine took that rule to heart and remembered it as best as she could ever since that day. But she has this feeling of being out of place somehow, and that when away from home she has no friends. For instance, when the family visits her grandparents, her grandmother gets her out of the way as soon as they arrive at the "Big House." Madelaine's grandmother tells her that she has to "earn her tea." While everybody else is having tea and scones and lemon cake, Grandmother puts Madelaine in the workroom all by herself. There, she has to fold pieces of paper that groceries were wrapped in, and stack these pieces in a shoebox. She also has to pull apart tangled bits of string that had tied up the groceries. When the untangling is done, she knots one end of string to the next piece of string, continuing until they are all joined into one long piece, which she then rolls into a ball. When Grandmother comes to see if Madelaine has done it all properly—and she did learn after her third try—Madelaine is so hungry and thirsty she doesn't care that Grandmother never says "thank you" or "well done," or anything warm like that.

On this day, Madelaine is interrupting her parents over their breakfast, with no idea what she wants from them and without even knowing if she believes they can help her. Madelaine stands near the corner of the table across which Dad and Mum usually hold hands. Before she can stop herself, words tumble out.

"I cannot go to that school anymore!" Her speaking and crying are mixed together in isiZulu and a little bit of English. Dad puts his arm around her shoulders and says she must go to that school until she is old enough to go to her sister's boarding school. Just like that.

Her mother coughs, wipes her mouth with a napkin, and does not look at Madelaine, who now believes both parents have not heard or understood her.

Madelaine tries again, more slowly this time. It is still not working. She makes them a deal. "I will return to school only if my friends Figele, nDugu, and Qala come with me."

Everything goes quiet; so quiet, she feels she must pop her ears like when driving down from the top of a high hill.

Her dad's voice is angry and cold: "No." He takes his arm away from her shoulders.

"Why can't I do that?"

"Because that would not be right."

"Why is it not right?"

She knows this behaviour is cheeky and rude, but just can't help it.

Her parents' answers take a long time. They are not angry anymore; they are just trying to calm her down. Madelaine knows they will not change their minds. Their long answer does not help her understand why it would not be right to bring her farm friends to school. Their answer feels untrue, as if there is something they are hiding.

Madelaine gives up trying and eventually arrives at school late, after the hand inspection. She feels lucky to miss it, but something about her parents' answer lingers.

She looks at the other pupils, at the colour of their eyes, their skin, their hair. They are all friends with each other. Most of them have blue eyes and blonde hair, and all of them, incsluding Miss

Barrie, have light skin. Madelaine thinks about Figele, nDugu, and Qala; how their hair grows differently than hers, and about the chocolate colour of their eyes. During recess, she goes to the mirror in the corner near the washbasin and stares at her eyes. They are blue. The skin on her arms is the colour of a bread crust. *Oh.*

I look a little bit like everyone else in school. These people who hate me; I look just like them! But, my hair is dark reddish brown and very curly—not blonde and straight. All this time I have been sure that I am an amaZulu girl, that I look like the people I love, know, and trust; that the reason nobody plays with or speaks to me at school is because they don't speak my language … but now?

That feeling in her belly—same as when she heard her brother's egg collection cracking under her bum—comes over her. But no, this is not the same as the egg-breaking time. That was a mistake, and she was punished for it. So, what is this feeling about? What mistake has she made this time? Could this be why Miss Barrie punishes her every morning? If so, Madelaine does not know what she has done wrong.

On their way home, Zondi answers her question about who she looks like, with a story about how the Great Spirit makes all things in nature to be their own kind. All living things were shown how to live together in their unique ways. She remembers Bazo also saying something like that.

"And," Zondi tells her, as they ride abreast on the shady path through the plantations, "then the Great Spirit made people, the woman different from man, each with gifts that made life better for everyone. As long as men and women have lived on this earth they have been learning to share. For some, this was not difficult to do, but those who came from far away brought a different way of living. This way we call 'dividing.' This dividing made a problem in the hearts and minds of all people.

"You see, *nTombi Yethu,* dividing is not the same as sharing. Sharing makes enough for everybody. Dividing does not do that. Dividing people from each other means that people look at each other and think, 'I am better than you, therefore I deserve more than you.' Yes, we are human. Yes, each one of us is different than the other, but we are all special in our own way, and each of us has a place in this world."

"A special place?"

Zondi thinks for a moment, places a hand over his heart, and remains silent. *This must be important.* His wise words usually come out as soon as she asks him something. Finally, he nods and says slowly, "Yes, that is so, *nTombi Yethu.* The special place is in here." He gently pats where his heart is.

Ah ... that is where the crying feeling starts. That is where the gladness starts when she sees him waiting for her after school. It is also the place she must keep calm so she can be strong when others divide her away from their group.

HOPE'S GLOVES

Madelaine follows her dad around, stands close to him, and asks to go with him in the pickup truck. Zondi had said she must talk to her father about these things she wants to understand: why she has no friends at school, why the teacher hits her hands every morning, and the meaning of "*kaffir*."

Madelaine likes the way her dad puts his big hand on her head when she stands close to him, and the way he lets her tag along, but he is always listening to somebody or talking to them. If she interrupts, he won't listen to her. Maybe she won't have to wait too long

One morning when there is no school, her dad says he is going to visit Great Aunt Grace and asks if she would like to go too.

"Oh, yes please!"

Aunt Grace is somebody Madelaine likes very much. Aunt Grace likes her, too. She knows this because Aunt Grace speaks in a way that makes her feel comfortable and loved, making it easy to remember her manners. She does not make Madelaine earn her tea.

Many years before Madelaine was born, Aunt Grace had a daughter named Hope, who died when she was seven years old. To help ease her sadness, Aunt Grace had a statue of Hope put in the garden, the size and age she was when she died. She is standing on tiptoe in bare feet. Her arms reach towards you. Flowers grow around her. Birds land on her fingers, on her curly hair, and hop and flutter to the birdbath next to her.

Madelaine knows that the statue reminds Aunt Grace of Hope, which makes her glad. She feels she knows Hope in a way that is difficult to describe.

As soon as her dad drives down the driveway on the way to her aunt's place, Madelaine tells him she wants to know about some things.

"What are these things you want to know about, my *Tombi*?"

"What does *kaffir* mean?"

"*Kaffir*? My *Tombi*, where did you hear that word?"

"From Miss Barrie at school. Um, she said it and some of the boys say it to me. And Miss Barrie, she hits my hands every day!"

"Your teacher hits your hands. What for? Hang on a moment; one thing at a time." He glances at her. "*Kaffir* is an unkind word; a word some people use to make others feel bad. It's used against those who have dark skin, my *Tombi*. We do not ever use that word."

"But why do Miss Barrie and the boys use that word about me? That's being unkind to me. Dad?"

"That's what it seems to be, but …"

"But, why? And why don't they talk to me, or even …" She was going to say "play with me," but remembered their way of playing was to corner her and try to rip her jodhpurs off. She didn't feel right talking about that.

"Talk to you, my *Tombi*? The other children don't talk to you?"

"No. Never. They only call me names. They talk to each other in that language called Afrikaans, and the other one … um … German."

In the rear-view mirror, the road disappears in a cloud of red dust. They pass closed gates, paddocks where horses are grazing, and farmhouses under big trees. They rumble over cattle grids and meander along roads that weave through plantations.

The next thing her dad says brings her back from watching the world pass by. Listening, she watches him; his set, firm jaw, strong, straight nose, and golden-reddish hair that blows in the wind rushing through the open windows. One tanned and muscled arm stretches to hold the steering wheel with a big, long-fingered hand—the hand that shows her how much she matters when he lays it gently on her head.

"My *Tombi*, I will try my best to explain a difficult thing to you. Are you ready?"

"Yes, I think so, Dad."

"I'll start with the other pupils at your school. Most of those boys, if not all of them, are sons of families that are angry about the outcome of the war. You see, my *Tombi*, they did not want our side to win. They were against our side before the war, and are against us still. They wanted Hitler to win, but we beat him. You are a daughter of the winning side. That could have something to do with why they are unkind to you.

"Their families built the school you go to. There was no school in the village before the war. That's why your sister and brother had a teacher at home—a governess. Do you understand what I am saying, my *Tombi*?"

Madelaine wants him to know that she understands about winning and losing, like her brother's rugby team and the polo teams her dad plays for—stuff like that, and about being a poor sport. She wants to tell him that she would be fine with a teacher coming to her home to teach her, but he is asking, "Why do you think Miss Barrie hits your hands every day?"

"I don't know. It feels like she is punishing me. I don't know what I've done!"

"Let's ask Aunt Grace about it, shall we?"

Aunt Grace must have been waiting for them, because as her dad parks the truck under some trees she comes out onto the veranda and waves. She is wearing a grey-blue dress, like the early morning mist, with a white lace collar and cuffs. Her black curly hair with streaks of grey is pinned up into a bun. Her smiling eyes are blue. She smells of lavender and her soft voice is warm and welcoming.

When the trio has finished their scones and jam, tiny cucumber sandwiches, and tea in delicate cups, Dad says it's time for him to see to things at the stables. He squeezes Madelaine's shoulder as he leaves the veranda and tells Aunt Grace he is sure she will be able to help Madelaine sort out a troubling question.

Madelaine is six years old and knows she is too big to sit on Aunt Grace's lap. But she wishes she could, to be closer to her kind ways. Instead, Madelaine leans towards her, noticing how that kindness appears; light shimmers around Aunt Grace, and it sparkles in her eyes.

"So, my girlie, tell me what is troubling you."

Madelaine blurts out that Miss Barrie is hitting her hands— usually only hers—every day and she doesn't know why.

Aunt Grace glances at her own hands, then at Madelaine's and asks, "Has Miss Barrie not told you why?"

"Uh, no ... not ever."

"Have you thought of asking her?"

All these questions about more questions make Madelaine feel small and frightened, but her aunt's kind voice reminds her that she is here across the tea table, asking for help from Aunt Grace.

"She tells me I have a *kaffir* tongue and she shouts when I don't understand her other language, and when she hits me she says things like 'dirty horses' and 'blacks,' and she doesn't stop the boys from chasing me and … um … oh no, Aunt Grace, I can't ask her that!"

"It's all right, my girlie, there, there. I am sure we will find a way to understand these troublesome things. I have a story to share that could help."

She passes her lace handkerchief to Madelaine. "Come, come now. Dry those tears, dearie."

Madelaine holds the delicate piece of lavender-scented cloth against her face and inhales deeply before wiping away her tears.

Aunt Grace begins her story by checking to see if Madelaine knows about the war and which side won, and that men and women from South Africa had trained to be soldiers to fight in that war.

She nods and Aunt Grace goes on to talk about a young woman who had become engaged to a young man, just before he left South Africa on a ship that took soldiers to Europe to fight. The young woman loved this soldier with all her heart and was sure he would come to no harm and return home for their wedding. When she received news that he was missing in action, she kept her hope alive, because missing in action could mean that he had not been killed—he just had not been found

"The sad thing is, my girlie, that when the war was over this young woman still had no news of her fiancé … until just a little while ago."

"Oh … ?"

"He was killed in the war."

"Oh. Do you know this lady, Aunt Grace?"

"Yes, I do. And so do you."

"I do?"

"She is your teacher, Miss Barrie."

Madeleine's eyes opened wide in surprise.

"Now, we need to think carefully about how we can stop her from hitting your hands. We must think about compassion."

Compassion? How can I feel compassion for somebody who hits me and shouts at me? Is this another rule for girls? Just when I thought Aunt Grace would tell me how to make everything better, she says this thing about compassion. I can't show compassion for my mother who seems to be broken down, because she does not want me to be close to her. I did not show compassion for the nurse when she was living in my home … she is a girl, so is the teacher, and so am I. My mother and my sister are girls, too. And Aunt Grace. This is hard, and feels so unfair.

Feeling that being a girl is not such a good thing now, Madelaine tries to listen.

"What would happen if you wore gloves on your rides to school?"

Gloves? And just like the first sip of Aunt Grace's sweet milky tea that tastes so good you want more, Madelaine feels this idea could be good, too. She asks Aunt Grace to tell her more about the gloves.

They leave the tea table and walk hand in hand down a long passageway, pass many doors, and finally stop at one, which Aunt Grace opens. She releases Madeleine's hand and leads her into a little girl's bedroom. A china doll dressed in a pretty frock sits on a small bed that is covered with a lace bedspread. Paintings of faeries hang on the wall over the bed. *Is this Hope's room?*

Madelaine's skin tingles. She could be a drop of dew full of the colours of her thoughts. That is how it feels to be in this room. Aunt Grace opens and closes a dresser drawer. She stands with her back to Madelaine, holding something in her trembling hands. Slowly, she turns around and presents a pair of dark blue leather gloves. "Here you are, my girlie. A pair of gloves for you."

Madelaine wriggles and pushes her fingers into soft places that she is sure were made just for her. The gloves fit perfectly. Hope had never worn them, because she died before she grew into them.

"You see, my girlie, if you wear these gloves on your rides to school, Miss Barrie will have no reason to hit your hands ever again."

Aunt Grace was right. The very next day Madelaine wears the gloves on her ride to school. She puts them away in her satchel before going anywhere near the other pupils.

At hand inspection time Miss Barrie is ready with her ruler. Madelaine is ready too, with clean hands lying flat on the desk. She is watching Miss Barrie's face.

That red lipstick mouth untwists into a thin red line as if she has sucked her lips into her mouth. The mean, sharp expression in her eyes changes to one of emptiness. Miss Barrie snorts through her nose and moves to the next pupil.

A new feeling wells up inside from where Madelaine knows her gladness and crying come: the feeling that Aunt Grace calls compassion. A big wave of thankfulness washes over her and fills her right up.

Madelaine knows she can't help Miss Barrie, but Aunt Grace has certainly helped her learn a new rule she can obey. Like Zondi said: "There's no sense in following the path of fear and hatred. Make that a rule for yourself, and never break it."

RULES FOR GIRLS

1946–1957

Being the only girl in school turns out to be fun when Madelaine is given the part of the bride in the Christmas play. She loves to sing, and the play is a musical. Having no teeth is not a problem.

They rehearse in the community hall just down the road from the school. So, for many days before the big day, the pupils don't have to be in school at their desks. Instead, they are at the hall.

It is a big hall in the middle of a field, and it has a stage with old dusty curtains that open and close as someone pulls on a rope. Aunt Grace plays the piano and teaches them the songs. Miss Barrie shows them how to walk onstage and where to stand.

The play is about the youngest daughter of a king, in a long ago time, who falls in love with a soldier from a poor family. When the soldier returns from fighting, the king permits them to be married. The songs that Aunt Grace teaches them tell the story about the day of their wedding.

Madelaine likes her bride dress. It is made from soft white material, and has a full skirt that falls to her feet. She does not like the crown she has to wear though. It is a circle of wire with paper flowers stuck to it, and will not stay on her head of curly hair properly.

The soldier's costume consists of dark blue pants and a short red jacket with many shiny buttons sewed on the front. The boy who plays the king wears a golden crown and an embroidered cloak. The rest of the boys play wedding guests. Their old-fashioned baggy costumes are made of rough material and show that they are farm workers; peasants, so Miss Barrie says.

The Saturday afternoon of the performance is a really hot day and everybody hopes that a thunderstorm does not keep the audience away. It seems as if the whole village has been invited; the bank manager, the doctor and his wife (who is also the nurse), storekeepers, the hotel owner, railway station master, blacksmith, farming families, and even Zilli, Bazo, and Zondi. They are allowed to stand at the back of the hall.

While waiting backstage for Aunt Grace to play the opening chords that will let the audience know the play is about to begin, Madelaine can smell tobacco smoke, horse dung, and field grass that was cut that morning. The chinking sound of teacups being laid out combines with chairs scraping across the floor, and voices of people talking and laughing. Music begins as the curtains open slowly.

The bride and the soldier hold hands and begin to walk towards the king who is seated on his throne, when the soldier pees his pants. He whispers to Madelaine that his pants are wet and that they should turn around and leave.

Oh no. Keep going! Besides, I have to sing any minute now.

With the same hand that is holding the soldier's, she grasps her skirt and lifts it high enough to cover the front of his pants. They keep walking towards the king, except now the soldier's arm is bent towards his stomach. He has to stay really close to Madelaine who is now singing. They shuffle against each other's feet until they finally reach the king. There are *oohs* and *ahhs* from the audience.

Have they noticed the soldier's wet pants?

By the time the peasants have knelt before the king and the cast is singing a song of happiness, the soldier's pants are dry enough for Madelaine to let go of her skirt.

To take the first bow, the cast and Miss Barrie form a line facing the audience. As instructed in rehearsal, each pupil must hold the hand of the person beside them and bow. They bow to shouts, whistles, and heavy applause.

Madelaine's crown slips and covers her eyes. She tries to free a hand from the soldier on one side, unsuccessfully, then from the king on the other side. The harder she pulls, the tighter they each hold her hand. It is time for the second bow. This time she bows lower and shakes her head. The crown falls with a *thunk* onto the wooden stage, rolls a short distance, topples over, and lies still. The performers straighten up and then, at last, the third and final bow. Aunt Grace plays the piano with all her heart. Madelaine doesn't mind that she lost her crown.

Perhaps the decision to send Madelaine to boarding school when she was eight years old was precipitated by the situation at the village school. She was not certain of that because unpleasant issues were not discussed in her family, and young children were expected to rally to changes brought about by adult family members without complaint.

Compared with the village school, she had entered a world populated entirely with girls—two hundred girls. The youngest was five and the seniors were seventeen and eighteen.

Zondi's companionship and counsel, and their rides through the plantations, became a treasured memory. Bazo and Zilli continued to maintain the household and serve her parents. Madelaine's jodhpurs and boots were only worn during holidays from school.

She now wore summer uniforms composed of cotton summer dresses printed with blue bells, with hemlines that reached just below the knee, and white socks and brown leather lace-up shoes that she polished. All the girls were expected to polish their shoes. Winter uniforms were made up of box-pleated, square-necked navy serge tunics, held by a saffron sash and worn over a long-sleeved shirt. They all were expected to wear white Panama hats in summer and navy wool berets in winter. Even underwear was regulated: navy flannel bloomers in winter and white cotton bloomers in summer. Girls in the pre-brassiere stage wore an undershirt until their breasts were large enough for a bra, which was chosen by the matron.

Wearing a uniform simplified life for many of the girls. Madelaine, who had never taken interest in dresses or had the desire to choose what to wear, accepted most aspects of wearing a uniform except for the bloomers; ugly and voluminous things, they were also uncomfortable, with sturdy elastic around the thighs and waist. She missed her handmade underwear; light, soft cotton that was loose around her crotch and groin.

As a way of controlling her thick and wildly curly hair, the school's barber chopped it short. No girl's hair was to touch her shirt collar unless it was long enough to braid. Madelaine's hair seemed to be unbraidable.

Her teeth were growing well, except for the two front teeth that were crooked. She had come to accept that trying to be pretty was a lost cause, and instead concentrated on being intelligent and interested in learning.

Her life became circumscribed by the bell that rang for every change in the daily routine, such as the first bell at half past five in the morning, rousing everyone in their dormitories. They rose early to take ten-minute baths, one girl after another, mostly in cold water. Then they got dressed and made their beds ready for inspection by the matron. The seven o'clock bell was their summons to the dining hall for breakfast. And so the day continually progressed to the sound of a bell.

Overwhelmed by this immersion into a female population that followed ways that were incomprehensible to her, Madelaine would disappear into one of the many piano practice rooms to find solitude, while herds of girls engaged in free social time after the day's lessons. The advantage of hiding in a practice room was the opportunity to use the piano, to play and practise the pieces she was learning.

Ever since the day—at around four years of age—of her discovery that she could compose music by making drawings in the earth at the edge of the driveway (drawings of shapes that the garden sounds evoked), and holding the picture of those shapes in her head while running back to the piano to play the shapes, she knew she loved music. Fortunately for Madelaine, her piano teacher came to recognize her gift, but not before a confrontation.

Madelaine's gift for music was in her acute ability to play by ear; sight-reading was difficult. She was not aware of this at the time, and perhaps neither was her teacher—until the day the teacher played a new piece, and instructed Madelaine to sight-read it. Madelaine sat down at the piano, hands poised over the keys, and barely glancing at the pages played what she had memorized by ear. The next thing she knew, the teacher's baton slammed down on her hands.

Enraged, Madelaine quickly stood, picked up her leather music case, and with her heart thundering and eyes burning and memories of Miss Barrie roaring through her mind, walked unsteadily to the door. She stopped, turned around and said, "I can't learn like that. I want you to teach me, but not like that. You know where to find me."

She was nine years old. Soon after that, Madelaine was called to the principal's office where she found both the principal and her piano teacher waiting. Since storming out of the music room, Madelaine had wondered if she would be punished for being rude and insubordinate, and what the punishment might be. Now, she was facing two strict women who could make her life miserable if they wanted to. She had, after all, broken one of the rules for girls: you do not refuse the voice of authority. And yet, Madelaine was uncowed.

"Madelaine, I assume you know why you have been called to my office," the principal said.

"I think I do m'Lady."

"Your teacher tells me you behaved in a manner unfitting for a girl of our esteemed establishment. What do you have to say about that?"

"M'Lady, I want to learn, but what my teacher did does not help me do that."

"I see. How would you explain that to your teacher?"

Madelaine turned to look at her piano teacher. A faint smile played at the corners of her lips and her beautiful piano-playing hands rested on her thighs, giving the impression of gentleness that Madelaine wanted so much to be real.

"M'Lady," she told the principal, "I cannot learn when I am hit with a stick."

"Oh, I see. How would you learn, then?"

Madelaine was still watching the piano teacher, hoping she would answer the question. She did, but in a way that surprised Madelaine.

"Rather than three afternoons a week for your lessons," she began, "I suggest five; two of which you will be playing by ear. The principal has agreed to this and gives you permission to miss field hockey."

Oh, that's wonderful! I don't like hockey. Wow!

And Madelaine, as demurely as she could, thanked the two women.

The principal had more to say. "From now on, Madelaine, rather than the hour's practice you have before breakfast in the practice room, you will practise on the piano in my drawing room."

Oh my! I love that grand piano. But wait ... this isn't a trap, is it?

No, the principal's instruction was not a trap. It was, for Madelaine, an introduction to the power women in authority can wield, particularly when, as in this instance, a sense of possibility is offered in conjunction with an opportunity to learn a new kind of responsibility—one towards being heard and not punished for speaking out.

Thus, Madelaine's morning routine changed. By six o'clock, she was tapping on the door of the small, private kitchen adjacent to the drawing room. Hettie, the principal's maid, would open the door and offer a cup of tea and tiny sandwiches left over from the previous night's meeting.

Hettie was a Zulu woman, a tall, big-boned, warm-hearted person whom Madelaine loved. Madelaine and Hettie buoyed each other's spirit and recognized how fortunate they were to be able to meet five mornings a week, and to speak isiZulu for the few minutes preceding the piano practice Madelaine enjoyed. The drawing room, furnished with a couch and armchairs upholstered in floral linen, smelled like home: faint traces of tobacco smoke, fresh flowers, and lavender-scented furniture polish. Madelaine was overjoyed by her good fortune, a feeling that carried her through the repetitive routine of boarding school days.

At the beginning of her final year at boarding school, the year Madelaine turned seventeen, she began to search for a university or college where she could study Early Childhood Education. Encouraged by the principal to attend a training institution in Cape Town, she announced her plan to her parents with great excitement.

"Oh, really? But you're far too young to leave home for somewhere so far away!" Her mother's disapproval was stingingly curt.

"But Mum, I would do well. I know I would. Imagine learning about children and working with music and songs and art … and I could work anywhere in the world after I get my degree!"

"No, it's not a good idea." Mum turned to Dad for his support in denying Madelaine the opportunity she longed to fulfill.

"Well, my *Tombi*, your mother could be right about you being too young. I'm certain you'd do well, but you'll do even better … let's say, in another year's time. Cape Town is a couple of thousand miles from here—quite far, I'd say."

"I don't want to wait a year—please don't make me do that. And, anyway, what would I do for a whole year while waiting?"

"There's plenty for you to do. For one thing, you could learn some lady-like ways of behaving … ways to polish you, shape you, and prepare you for marriage, for instance."

Madelaine's spirit quailed at the prospect. She pictured herself trapped in hats and gloves selected for the right occasion, making stilted conversation with disapproving ladies over tea, engaging in politely chaste exchanges with young marriageable farmers. Oh, no! Imagine being shaped for that.

Rather than continuing with this discussion that she knew would only make her mother more obdurate, she pondered over the possibility of speaking to people who might influence her parents to reconsider.

Using her favourite fountain pen she wrote letters to three people on her best notepaper. Aunt Grace, having offered consistent support to Madelaine since childhood (Hope's gloves, for instance), was the first to come to mind. Madelaine explained her hopeful plans, asking Aunt Grace for her thoughts about Madelaine's desire to further her education.

Although His Eminence the Archbishop had, at times, intimidated Madelaine, she remembered him complimenting her on her angelic voice when she sang solo in the cathedral. The letter she wrote to him, although more formal than her letter to Aunt Grace, was no less clear about her hopeful plans.

And then she wrote to an uncle who was a member of parliament. She liked him and his easy conversation, as well as the interest he took in how young people viewed the world.

His Eminence the Archbishop replied swiftly with an invitation to tea.

Aunt Grace's reply followed. She agreed with Madelaine's plans and promised to speak to her parents. The uncle's secretary wrote to say he would be in the area in a week's time and would speak to Madelaine then.

"Your Eminence. Thank you for inviting me to tea."

"Well, m'dear, your letter is not to be ignored, but I am curious about something. Let us go through to my office. We'll take our tea there and discuss your plans."

On his desk, a tray laid with a large teapot covered in a knitted wool cosy, milk jug, bowl of sugar, a plate of chocolate digestive biscuits, and two fine china teacups waited for them. His Eminence lowered his tall bulk of a body into a leather armchair while waving his hand to a dainty upright chair to indicate where Madelaine should sit.

"Would you pour, please? I take mine black."

Madelaine went through the motions of pouring tea and offering biscuits before she settled herself on the dainty chair.

"Now. What I'm curious about is this: Do your parents know that you have written to me?"

"No, Your Eminence, they do not."

"And why is that?" His mane of snow-white hair shifted as he turned his head the better to meet Madelaine's eyes. She tried not to flinch under his direct gaze.

"They would prefer me to wait a year before going to Cape Town to further my education because I'm too young—and besides, Your Eminence, my mother insists I'd learn lady-like ways by staying at home. And I thought that I'd seek your eminent advice before broaching the subject again with them."

"I see. When will you tell them that we have met?"

"When your guidance and advice provide direction for me, Your Eminence."

He held out his empty cup to Madelaine who instantly stood to take it from him while offering him more, which he accepted.

"I hear from your lady principal that you do well in most subjects, and that you show great promise as an innovator—albeit with a strong will." The corner of his mouth twitched with the ghost of a smile and his eyes twinkled. *Oh no*, thought Madelaine, *he probably knows about the altercation I had with the music teacher.* Madelaine remained mute and lowered her eyes to her cup. She tried to breathe calmly.

"Am I the only person to whom you've written a letter outlining your hopes and plans?"

Madelaine told him about Aunt Grace and her uncle, the MP.

"Ah—then this is what we're going to do. I will invite your Aunt Grace and your uncle to join me here to talk over your plans. Meanwhile, I think you'd best tell your parents about your letters and explain that I, your Aunt Grace, and your uncle will meet with them in the very near future."

Madelaine's trust, she discovered, had not been misplaced when, after a month or so on a long weekend home from school, she and her parents had a conversation.

"I'm still not certain I like the manner by which you've gone about getting your way, Madelaine. Fancy going as far as persuading others to support your plan ... I mean—really! His Eminence! How can I refuse him?" Her mother was clearly upset, but Madelaine was not. She also was not interested in explaining her reasons.

"*Tombi*, after hearing three sides to your hopes to go on with learning, I can't stop you, and actually don't even want to. You should go ahead and apply to that place in Cape Town. Let's take it from there. Good?"

And so it was a triumphant leap into the beginning of a new life far from home.

NATURE? SHE IS A VANDAL!

1961

Madelaine marries William five months before her twenty-first birthday, three months after she and Will graduated from university. Within days of their wedding she and Will are aboard a ship sailing from South Africa, across the Atlantic Ocean to Rio de Janeiro.

They move into a small apartment between Ipanema and Copacabana. Although Madelaine has no experience with apartment living, having grown up in a seventeen-room home on a large farm in South Africa, life feels daring and full of possibility with the intense thrill of a new culture. Will has begun work with a group of architects and Madelaine's interest in opening an English immersion preschool has caught the attention of the British Council.

Late one afternoon, Madelaine, Will, and his colleagues meet in a beachside bar in Copacabana. They sip cold amber beer amidst the glow of a sun that is slipping into a turquoise, satin-like sea. A breeze licks her hot cheeks and ignites a spark that flames her desire to celebrate her twenty-first birthday.

She is in love with life, with Will, and with her freedom from South Africa's racist laws and her family's disapproval. The cementing of new friendships urges her to raise a glass to announce her upcoming birthday.

Enthusiastic responses almost bowl her over. "Celebration! A milestone. Girl becomes woman … finds her own path …"

But, where to celebrate?

Ideas, bizarre and fabulous, swirl around the table: rent a nightclub, live jazz, float the party on a barge in the bay, a street party. More beer and platters of grilled prawns in garlic butter are served. With conversation woven together by Italian, Portuguese, German, English, sips of beer, and lips smacking of buttery garlic, her table companions finally reach a consensus: a villa, situated on five acres of parkland in the city of Rio.

During the 1920s, the young and ambitious son of a wealthy tycoon went in search of a wife after inheriting his father's considerable fortune. While conducting business in Italy, he attended the opera *Madama Butterfly*, in the company of the rich and elite. By the time the final curtain closed, he had become so besotted with Mimi that, upon meeting her at the after party, proposed marriage.

She was hesitant about leaving her native Naples to live in Rio de Janeiro, but did ask him to wait for what she promised would be a satisfying answer. Secure with the knowledge that he had won her over, he returned to Rio de Janeiro aspiring to build a home and design gardens that would reflect her beauty and his undying love—the very villa under discussion around Madelaine's table laden with beer and prawns.

The opera star accepted the man's proposal, they married, and she moved into the villa he'd built for her. The couple enjoyed decades of extravagant splendour, and they hosted legendary soirées and glamorous events attended by the world's most famous and notorious. It was said that more often than not, guests were obliged to check in their pistols and diamond tiaras upon arrival.

A debate arises with Madelaine's dining companions about why this man lost his fortune, and about the cause of his disappearance. The romantics believe his adored wife died of an undisclosed illness, breaking his heart and forcing him into loose and careless ways. Others presumed the couple ran away to avoid paying debts incurred over the years, or that she, fed up with his philandering, returned to Naples. He followed her and was "dispatched" by the Mafia.

All they knew for certain was that he lost his fortune, abandoned his estate, and disappeared. The Municipality of Rio appropriated the property, sold the contents, locked the villa, and appointed a caretaker.

"Abandoned and unoccupied for longer than a decade?" Madelaine asks.

"Not a problem," someone reassures her, and goes on to explain that their employer, an architect, has entered a competition to submit a design that would best utilize the estate site. Their office has a key to the main gates and the telephone number of the caretaker.

So, on a warm and tender spring morning, Will drives her to the villa in his 1957 silver convertible MG sports car with the top down. From a busy four-lane street, he turns into what she believes is a parking bay, until they stop at a pair of impressive wrought-iron gates supported by two stone pillars, each flanked by a winged lion. Imperial palms line the driveway; their trunks rise hundreds of feet and appear to hold up their fronds as an offering to the sky. The car brushes by gigantic overgrown shrubs, some with blooms the size of dinner plates. The weight of foraging bees moves petals, which filters sunlight into patches of breathing colour that float on her bare arms. Dappled light dances between the trunks of palms like hosts of faeries.

They stop at the front entrance where steps, built in decreasing semicircles, are reminiscent of an elaborate ball gown sweeping up to a cinched waist. At the top step rises an ornate wrought-iron gate entwined by an overgrown bougainvillea. A wall of scarlet and coral-toned flowers blocks the entrance. Grasses grow through cracks between the stones underfoot. Lizards scuttle away.

A man carrying a shotgun and accompanied by three dogs appears at the far side of the building. Will greets him as Senor Gabriel.

Gabriel signals the dogs to stay, lays down the shotgun beside them, and approaches Madelaine and Will, who are waiting on the top step. He has dark, curly hair that is greying at the temples. The sleeves of his faded blue shirt, rolled up to his elbows, show lean and sinewy forearms. Black slacks fit comfortably across his narrow hips. On his feet are black leather sandals.

His gestures are restrained and considered, his posture erect. Madelaine watches closely as Gabriel selects a key from a ring of many large keys, moves tendrils of bougainvillea away from the keyhole and unlocks the gate. He casts a despairing look at the overhang of growth. Then, squaring his shoulders and bracing his feet, takes hold of the gate and heaves it open. Bougainvillea branches snap and tear away from the structure, showering them with leaves and flowers.

Madelaine's hoot of delight is cut off by Gabriel telling them that before he allows them to cross the threshold, they are to understand he will show only the Diva's rooms and some of the gardens.

Ah, the Diva. Madelaine steps into a marble-floored foyer flanked by a deep recess on each side, barricaded by iron-barred gates. Could this have been where the diamond tiaras and pistols were handed over at those legendary soirées?

Gabriel leads them through an arch, across a band of shade, and into a sunlit courtyard, in the centre of which yawns an empty swimming pool, its faded interior sloping to a floor where flakes of aquamarine paint, twigs, and papery petals shift and rustle in the light spring breeze. Clay urns arranged around the pool tilt at dizzying angles. Hairy, finger-like roots have crept through cracks to wrap themselves around the urns, holding them intact.

Straggling along after Gabriel, their footsteps sounding like an intrusion into the enormous silence, they join him at a pair of closed doors. His head is inclined at a reverential angle as he selects a key and slides it into the keyhole. He turns to look at the visitors to make certain, Madelaine thinks, that they too revere the Diva and will show respect for her quarters. She nods her understanding. Satisfied, he swings open both doors as if announcing, "Señora. *Cara mia.*"[5]

They ascend a set of marble stairs that curves at a sunlit landing. Gabriel motions them into a spacious room devoid of furniture. And yet, there is a sense of fullness in the room. Textured light ripples across ceilings the colour of a dawn sky speckled with faded golden stars. Walls are alive with artists' renditions of maidens wearing wisps of cloth, some with satyrs in pursuit, others caught in tender embraces. Fingers of light stream between the leaves of a vine that clings to the outer side of an oval window and caress a dove-grey marble floor.

Gabriel clears his throat. "We stand in the Diva's bedroom now."

A rush of excitement explodes across Madeline's hips. She raises her arms to embrace the air, to kiss the light, imagining herself prancing with the maidens flitting across the walls and

5   my darling (Italian)

ponders the orgasmic energy present in this bedroom. Gabriel glances furtively in her direction, as if experiencing a similar lust. Swayed by her look, he leads them into "the room where the Diva bathed and dressed."

Deeper shades of paint on the walls indicate where enormous mirrors had once hung—mirrors that must have fetched a considerable sum when the city liquidated the villa's assets. The original colour of the walls preserved and shaped by the mirrors—that of crushed red roses—seems to kiss the lines that meet a floor of shell-pink marble. An oval black marble bathtub on a raised dais sits across from where Madelaine is standing. *Ah, the Diva bathing with her besotted husband in a room suffused in the hues of a passionate heart.*

Madelaine is certain of Gabriel's private and undying passion for the Diva. It seems important to his dignity that he keep his emotions hidden, because he brusquely ushers them from this sumptuous boudoir, locking the doors in a manner that implies he has left his feelings locked behind them.

This sets her to wondering how he might feel about opening the villa for a small soirée. Perhaps he prefers to live quietly within his thoughts and secret desires. Given the scant number of people she would invite, it would be a small gathering of those respectful of the Diva.

Gabriel quickens his pace, moving past the empty swimming pool, through the gate overhung with ravaged bougainvillea, and down the stone steps towards the dogs and his shotgun. Surprisingly, Gabriel ignores them and veers off towards the gardens.

Snatches of sounds, some reminiscent of sighs, accompany them; others evoke images of golden ripe peaches and purple grapes dripping with juice. Atmospheric pockets thicken the air, seeking her attention, playfully slowing her down. She glances over her shoulder, catches a glimpse of a tennis court carpeted with flowering weeds, and distracted, is unaware of entering a dark, leafy canopy until she bumps into Gabriel.

He is clearly angry, cursing under his breath and shaking his fist at what remains of a greenhouse. Metal frames twist crazily skyward, broken glass glitters at her feet, and shards of terracotta have been flung in all directions. She notices that plants, having burst through their pots, are sending roots along and over the edges of shelves, across the floor of the greenhouse and through gaps in broken windowpanes. Vines and creepers in their upward surge to reach the light have literally gone through the roof, torn apart the boundaries of their cultivated civility, and taken back the garden. Madelaine is secretly delighted with this expression of unbridled vitality.

Gabriel, who from rigid frustration has crumpled into defeat, growls through gritted teeth, "Nature? She is a vandal!" He turns away from what Madelaine suspects he sees as a mess of broken glass that he must clean up and marches back to the villa.

Gabriel asks Madelaine to wait with his dogs and beckons to Will to walk with him. She watches them stroll away, teetering between the hope that Gabriel will agree to a small, simple gathering and apprehension that he will refuse their request. She had no idea of the enchantment an abandoned home could present, nor had she ever set foot in a love token of that magnitude.

The men turn and slowly make their way back to where Madelaine waits. They are smiling. Does that mean Gabriel has agreed?

He extends his hand to shake Madelaine's, looking directly into her eyes, a look that spoke more clearly and loudly than any words he might have spoken. Will is grinning widely. "It is agreed. The gathering will take place the night before your birthday."

Madelaine thanks Gabriel and they release their handshake. Arm in arm, Will and Madelaine walk towards the car, when Gabriel calls to them, "I trust you were aware of the absence of electricity in the villa."

The mention of electricity and the absence thereof reminds Madelaine of the countless times the generator on the farm in South Africa had broken down, making it necessary to light kerosene lanterns. Madelaine considers the traditional party her parents there would have arranged for her birthday, and feels somewhat like those plants that have burst through the bounds of their containment. A sense of having escaped into a new adventure overtakes her. The full impact of celebrating in a villa where echoing silence stirs up memories eager to be released into revelry makes her feel reckless.

She invites each person she met during that evening of beer and prawns and asks them to bring their friends. She collects glasses, buys hundreds of candles, a selection of cheeses, fruit, bread, and wine. Will makes arrangements to pick up blocks of ice and a keg of beer, and finds a battery for their portable record player. Gabriel, caught up in their enthusiasm, sweeps and fills the swimming pool. He also provides kerosene lanterns.

On the evening of the party, Madelaine, opting to go barefoot, wears a shift she made from soft muslin. Will has chosen a cotton shirt, slacks, and a panama hat. Gabriel, smartly dressed in a dark pinstriped suit and tie, stands at the open gate (having trimmed the overhanging bougainvillea) to welcome and usher guests and their friends into a world glowing amidst the light of candles and lanterns. Reflections from a heliotrope sky turn the pool into a jewel. Pergolesi's flute concerto wafts between arches of stone.

Guests find wine cooling in the black marble bathtub. Near boards of bread, cheeses, and fruit stands a keg of cold beer. They fill their glasses and raise them to Madelaine's milestone birthday, singing "Happy Birthday" in several languages, momentarily over-shadowing the sound of flutes and violins. Madelaine, overcome with shyness, turns her attention to the cracked urns at the pool-side, observing how they still tilt crazily while the surviving roots, underlit by candles, reach into the conviviality.

Someone puts bossa nova on the record player. Stan Getz and João Gilberto instantly have everyone dancing; hips gyrate, hair swings, arms rise, and people swirl, spin, twirl, and fall into each other's arms; around the pool and between pillars they dance. Couples shed clothing as they pass through the fringe of encircling candlelight, disappearing into alcoves, recesses, and the Diva's bedroom. Later, they return, naked and satiated, and slip into the pool, setting reflected starlight to dance on ripples that lap and smack at the edges.

Candles burn down into pools of wax. Gabriel leans against the arched threshold, bidding each guest a safe trip home. Pergolesi's flute concerto brings an air of the Renaissance era into their midst. Madelaine seems to be floating, so when Will tells her that he will be taking her for an intimate twosome in a nightclub at the Copacabana Palace Hotel on her birthday, where they will be entertained by Eartha Kitt and her band, she becomes airborne as if angels were lifting her into the dawn of a new age.

By the following evening, Madelaine has bought black stilet-tos for the occasion and has her hair done in a beehive style. She wears a strapless black dress cinched at the waist, and a full skirt of taffeta reaches to her knees. Her eyes are made up with mascara and eye pencil. Will wears a tan linen suit, crisp white shirt, and purple silk cravat.

The clear glass dance floor stretches across a pond of golden carp, where frill-finned orange fish swim through bands of light that illuminate the floor and the dancers' feet. Eartha Kitt's voice propels Madelaine from her seat at their table for two. So drawn is she to Eartha's voice, and by the idea of dancing on underlit glass, for a moment she forgets her husband and steps onto the floor.

As if coming out of a trance, she is suddenly aware that other dancers have stepped aside to give her the floor. She catches Will's eyes. He strokes his goatee and raises a glass of champagne to her. She dances solo to Eartha and the band playing, "Ain't Misbehavin.'"

Indeed.

PEACOCKS IN THE RAIN

In the spring of 1962, Madelaine had been living in Rio de Janeiro for a year and a half, and was about to celebrate her twenty-second birthday when a cablegram from her father in South Africa arrived. Expecting birthday wishes, she opened the brown envelope with a feeling of happiness, believing she'd been remembered by her parents who, just eighteen months ago, had reluctantly allowed her to marry and embark on a ship voyage to Rio de Janeiro.

The message from her father carried no birthday wishes. Instead, it stated that she was needed at home by her mother, and to come as soon as possible.

Cablegrams were cryptic at the best of times, and telephoning from Brazil to a party line in rural South Africa was not possible.

Her mother had been unwell as far back as Madelaine could recall. She suffered from long drawn-out spells of depression, during which she laid in bed behind a closed door, effectively removed from contact with her children, particularly her youngest, Madelaine, born several years after her sister and brother.

The belief that had taken hold when Madelaine was a small child continued to lurk in the corners of her mind, often eroding her confidence; the belief that it was her fault her mother was sick and remote. To overcome this, Madelaine had edged closer to a state of trying not to care … too much.

Her father's summons felt like a demand, that she was to drop everything and step out of her life of purpose and engagement. Then again, going home to see her mother could provide an opportunity to understand why she believed her mother's sickness was her fault. Spending time with her mother might ease that dull ache in Madelaine's heart, which sometimes woke her at night. Madelaine replied to her father's cablegram and was soon on a flight home to Durban, South Africa.

The plane circled over Rio before leaving the continent of South America, offering her first aerial view of the city she had grown to love. White sandy beaches of Copacabana and Ipanema frilled with frothy waves travelled with the breeze. Sugar Loaf Mountain and the statue of Christ the Redeemer atop Corcovado Mountain overlooked favelas that spilled down hillsides like a collection of discarded treasures. The crowded landscape of Rio behind her, the vast openness of the Atlantic Ocean suddenly presented her reflection in the window of the plane. Curls framing her face were an unruly spray above dark, well-defined eyebrows and wide-set eyes. The freckles on her nose were not visible in the reflection, but her lips closed in quiet contemplation were as prominent as the determined set of her chin.

I look like my mother, but am certain I don't feel as she does. Maybe there's something she has always needed from me that I'm not aware of. She could have shown me, instead of treating me as someone lacking … lacking what, though … a sense of duty?

How does a child learn to be dutiful?

My older sister is a dutiful daughter; adult family members pro-claim that with pride. My older brother seems to function with a differ-ent set of rules when it comes to being dutiful—perhaps because he is a son. And then there's me, the youngest by several years, the late lamb, as my Irish relatives dubbed me.

Madelaine's father met her at the Durban airport, but instead of taking the route towards home on the farm, he drove into the city.

He spoke little, drummed his fingers on the steering wheel, heaved an exhausted sigh, and launched into explaining that her mother was in a psychiatric hospital recovering from another elec-tric shock treatment—the third over a period of about ten years, he reminded her.

Where had I been for the previous treatments? Oh yes, of course! At boarding school and university—a period of around eleven years. Ah, no wonder I don't remember.

"Perhaps this one will cure her, my girl."

"But what's the matter with her, Dad?"

"The doctors say it's manic depression. They believe that elec-trocuting her brain will make her better."

"Did electrocuting her brain the last two times make her better?"

"Uh, who's to say. Really. These newfangled cures ..." He brakes so a farm truck laden with bags of potatoes can make a turn, and then lights a cigarette.

Shrugging, he gives her a quick look. "All I can do is trust the doctors and hope for the best."

Madelaine notices sorrow beneath that stoic mask, which makes her think, *last resort*. She loves her dad: his voice, his tall, broad-shouldered, big-hearted manliness, long shapely fingers, and precise hands. In her estimation, he could solve anybody's problems with warmth, compassion, and a wry, gentle sense of humour.

"Thought you'd like to take a shower and change your clothes before seeing your mum, so we're going to The Club where you can freshen up. I'll have a drink while I wait."

"Good idea, Dad. Thanks."

The Club was a Victorian colonial institution established in the late 1800s, reserved exclusively for gentlemen and featuring guest rooms for wives and female family members.

Madelaine felt freshened up to a certain extent after a hot scented bath, a change of clothes, and a pot of tea. She had selected from her suitcase a pale yellow linen shirt and deep blue cotton slacks.

On their way to the hospital, he warned that the electric shock treatment had somewhat destroyed her mum's ability to recognize people.

I'm people? Really?

He dropped her off at the hospital entrance with directions to her mother's private room, a "stay strong" wink, and a promise that he would return in a while.

Madelaine, striding with purpose, tried not to rush down the corridor to her mother's room, to avoid arriving out of breath let alone flustered. She passed only three doors before arriving at her mother's room.

The door was open a crack. She tapped on it and in a muted singsong voice called out, "Hello Mum. It's me, Madelaine. May I come in?"

There was no response, unless the rustling sound of a body moving beneath bed sheets can be counted as an acknowledgement. Madelaine waited a heartbeat or two, then nudged the door open and entered the room.

Light streamed through a window on the far side of the narrow bed onto a highly polished wooden floor. The prone figure propped up by pillows and cast into shadow resembled a still-life pencil drawing on a stark white background.

Madelaine approached her mother who stirred, and then as if surfacing from the depths of some deep pool, raised her arms to offer an embrace. Greying curls were damp (with sweat?) and pinned away from bruised temples. Her arms were punctured with needle marks and there were dark purple stains on her wrists. Madelaine was deterred from the embrace. Instead, she gently grasped her mother's outstretched hands and looked into her eyes as she had done all her life. Yes, her mother's eyes were the familiar blue-grey colour that sparkled with an infectious delight on good days. Now, their hollow longing spoke of resignation, as if she had simply given up on life.

Madelaine's heart lurched. No matter how hard she tried to move into those arms, the resolve to manage without motherly connection—which she had perpetuated for twenty-two years—would not soften. Her resistance did not go unnoticed. A mist of sorrow clouded those grey-blue eyes as her mother tightened the hold she had on Madelaine's hands. She lowered her arms to rest on the sheet covering her thighs, thus drawing her daughter a step closer. This made it necessary for Madelaine to sit on the edge of the bed. Here, the smell of hospital, medicine, floor polish, and disinfected sheets assailed Madelaine, forcing her to hold her breath.

Across the distance between mother and daughter came, "What troubles you, my girl?"

No "Thank you for coming all that way," or "How lovely to see you"—nothing like that. Madelaine felt churlish for wanting acknowledgement, yet at the same time her mind balked and spun away from her mother's sad, questioning eyes and the sterile hospital room to crouch like a wild creature trapped in a small place, wary and afraid.

How can I answer that? She must know that I learned early in life to not bother her for love and reassurance.

Her mother's question did indicate recognition, though (she was not "people," after all), but it was too late now—too late to feel happy or relieved at being recognized. Madelaine's mind, having begun its retreat from her mother, fled back to a day in 1944 when she was four years old, a day when her mother had *not* recognized her little girl. Like a drop of blue ink landing in a bowl of milk, this memory flooded into every corner of her consciousness.

Madelaine is lying on her bed, where she is supposed to be having a nap. It is a hot summer afternoon—too hot to be outside in the fierce sun. Her garden spirit friends are resting. The birds are silent. Her older sister and brother are away at boarding school and Dad is away doing "war work." Her Zulu friends who look after her are off for the afternoon and her mum is in bed. She wonders where the nurse could be, because the house—aside from the tin roof pinging in the heat—is silent.

Her stomach hurts. She could be hungry, but doesn't feel like eating. Her bedroom, although it is a big room for one little girl, seems too small for what she is feeling. She cannot lie still; she tosses and turns, hums, counts her fingers, and watches the white curtains move in the breeze as if they are breathing. The fragrance of grapes ripening on the veranda mingles with the scent of freshly mowed lawns.

Madelaine climbs down from her bed and tiptoes to the door. It is open a crack. She peers up and down the passageway and then straight across to the door of one of the guest rooms. She knows her mum is in that room and wants to see her so badly she cannot think properly. Her mum has been in bed behind that door for so long, she can't remember when she last saw her. Nobody answers Madelaine's questions about why her mum stays in there, or why the nurse who looks after her forbids Madelaine from going anywhere near her.

Madelaine is scared of the nurse, with her crackling, white starched uniform with buttons that strain across her big bosom, her stringy grey hair tied in a bun behind her thick neck, and her huge arms and hands that reach to smack her, like the time Madelaine tried to sneak into that room and was caught. She was smacked over and over until she squirmed away from the hold the nurse had on her hair, and ran to hide in the hydrangeas.

Madelaine watches that door. It opens. Out comes a tray of dishes carried by the chunky nurse. The nurse hooks a foot around the door to pull it closed and stomps past Madelaine's door towards the kitchen. Madelaine waits. The nurse turns the corner into the passageway that will take her to the kitchen, and Madelaine makes a dash for the door behind which she believes her mum is imprisoned.

The door has not been latched. Madelaine nudges it open just a little, enough to let her small body squeeze through. Pink curtains are closed to the afternoon sun; the room glows as light in the depths of a conch shell would.

Madelaine first notices the profile of a woman's face. Black curly hair is flattened and damp, the corner of her mouth sadly pulls down towards the bottom of her cheek. This woman, propped up on white pillows, is her mum. One hand holds tightly to the sheet that covers her, while the other moves a palm-leaf fan in front of her face slowly from side to side, side to side.

Standing stock-still, Madelaine waits for any sign that would invite her to come closer to the bed—closer to Mum. Just to hold her hand, even; but there is no sign.

A mewling sound escapes through Madelaine's tightly closed lips. The fan stops moving and Mum looks in her direction. Madelaine wants to call out a greeting, but there is no spark of recognition in those eyes. Mum is looking at her as if she is a stranger. She does not know this little girl standing in the room.

Pee trickles down Madelaine's legs and puddles around her bare feet on the polished wooden floor. She can't breathe. Her feet squeak in the puddle of pee as she turns and runs from the room, down the passageway, out into the garden and past the tennis court, across the lawn in search of Zilli, her nanny and best friend.

She sees the shape of Zilli's tall, broad body sitting on the grass in the shade of a tree, the ochre rose colour of the soles of Zilli's feet, the dark glossy brown of her arms. She is cleaning silver cutlery and has laid the polished forks and spoons in neat rows on a white linen cloth beside her.

Madelaine trips over the gleaming forks and spoons, tumbles into Zilli's lap, and buries her face in her warm breasts, wailing; the breasts that had succoured her into life when Madelaine had been brought home from the hospital and, crying from hunger, was fed in tandem with Zilli's newborn daughter. Zilli holds her in the crook of her arm, tenderly wipes away Madelaine's tears with a polishing rag, and croons a loving song.

This long-buried memory of her mum lying in a rose-tinted room on a hot summer afternoon when she was four years old evaporated the instant her mother released Madelaine's hands. However, the emotions evoked by that memory continued to roil and rise: shame, fury, a sense of inadequacy, loss, and betrayal. She longed for her mother to offer a way through this emotional mine-field as fervently as she had longed for it in her childhood.

And yet, Madelaine knew that wishing for such a change would be fruitless, particularly in the present reality of her mother's weak-ened state.

She had not known how to love and support me as a child. Why would I expect that now, at age twenty-two?

Like the sound of a clapper slamming closed on a film set, signalling actors to action, Madelaine snapped from her internal battle into acceptance. Her young life had not been bereft of love and care, after all; only her mother had been inattentive.

"What troubles you, my girl?" her mother repeated.

Madelaine's response was tainted with mistrust. "Why did you ask for me to come home?"

Her mother looked down at the palms of her hands, inspected her nails, interlocked her fingers, and rested her hands on her stomach. Shaking her head, she rolled her lips into her mouth, closing them firmly like a small child refusing to take another spoonful of food.

Feeling compassion—empathy, even—was a struggle. Her mother's reaction to Madelaine's question sat like a stone in her gut.

During Madelaine's years at boarding school her mother had often asked her to come home for a visit. Madelaine was young and had an innocent desire to fulfill her duty as a daughter, to help her mother feel better. The requests (or were they demands?) began when Madelaine was twelve years old and continued until her final year at boarding school, when she turned seventeen.

Her dad phoned the headmistress to gain permission for Madelaine to be absent from school for a couple of days. Then either he or the chauffeur would pick her up and drive the hour or so home to her mother on the farm. Most often, Madelaine would find her in bed—the enormous double bed her parents shared—with her bedside light on regardless of the time. Next to the lamp were her Gold Leaf cigarettes and matches, a crystal jug of water covered by a beaded circle of netting, a tumbler, and a bottle of painkillers.

Zilli had become her mother's caretaker by then and was utterly relied upon to draw baths, tend fires, bring trays of tea, and on the days when Mum felt well enough to leave her bed, deliver freshly washed and ironed clothes. When summer storms laden with thunder and lightning drew close, Zilli and Mum kept each other company, hiding under the bed until the storm passed.

A ritual formed around these visits from boarding school. She opened all the curtains in her parent's bedroom, the living room, dining room, and her dad's den. The front and back door were opened to draw fresh air through the heart of their home. After accomplishing all this, she collected the flower clippers and a basket and picked as many flowers as she could carry. Madelaine arranged the flowers in vases and bowls, placing some in her parent's bedroom and the rest in the living room and dining room. Then it was time for Madelaine to play the piano. Although her visits home did not consistently improve her mother's state of mind, Madelaine at least believed she had performed her daughterly duties as best as possible.

Madelaine rose from the edge of her mother's hospital bed, desperate to clear the suffocating stillness that had thickened the air and to dislodge the stone in her gut.

Ah. Music would brighten the atmosphere.

"Do you hear songs in your mind, Mum?"

As a response to this question, her mother began to sing the Twenty-Third Psalm and Madelaine joined her. When her mother lost the words, Madelaine reached for her hand and kept singing. Together they sang to the end of the second verse and then her mother asked, "Do you remember singing that solo in the cathedral?"

"Yes, Mum, I do."

"It is no wonder the congregation thought an angel was singing."

That remark was soothing to Madelaine's soul.

Her mother began humming "My Blue Heaven," a tune she had often played on the piano. At one point, her mother's singing slowed expectantly, and as Madelaine had done as a child she changed the words to, "Just Daddy, and me, and Mummy makes three."

As a sunbeam finds its way through fog, a sparkle shone in her mother's eyes. Her hands patted the beat on her thighs, and her feet moved with phantom-like dance steps.

Emboldened now, Madelaine finds herself thinking about superstitions. Many signified impending disaster: spilling salt on the dining table, for example. If a few granules are not immediately pinched between the thumb and forefinger of the right hand and tossed over the left shoulder, an insulted God of Plenty would unleash the punishment of famine. Also, if a bird flew into the house, prepare for the death of a loved one. One particular superstition, though, uppermost in Madelaine's mind, was her mother's reaction to peacock feathers.

Madelaine is around six or seven years old and has recently learned how to ride a bicycle. She often pedals down their long driveway lined with flowering trees, across a dirt road, and along Tompie's long driveway lined with deodar cedar trees. Edith Thompson is her real name. She is an old woman with curly silver hair and blue eyes that shine with kindness. With her children all grown up and her husband passed on, she lives alone in a stone and brick farmhouse with a deep wraparound veranda. Madelaine is certain of a warm welcome whenever she hops off her bike at the front steps leading to Tompie's veranda. She might find Tompie reading, but most often she is working in her extensive gardens.

Tompie and Madelaine get on very well, mostly because they both speak to animals, flowers, plants, birds, and insects and understand what they are saying. Soon after arriving, Tompie offers what she calls a lazy tea: homemade slices of bread that are cut into small squares and topped with butter, tomato, and watercress. They take their tea in china cups with matching saucers and hold conversations about faeries and garden spirits.

A gigantic magnolia tree grows in a field where Tompie's mares and foals graze. One day this tree, with thick limbs that spread far enough to create a wide circle of shade for the horses, comes alive with magic for Madelaine when she discovers Tompie's peacocks roosting on the tree's lower branches instead of sitting on the ground or foraging in the field grasses. Tompie's explanation that the peacocks roost on the lower branches when a rainstorm is on its way in no way diminishes the magic for Madelaine and further sparks her young imagination.

She supposes that these large birds know they are protected from the rain while taking cover under the magnolia's big, green, waxy leaves, and that the purpose of the fleshy, moon-coloured petals of the magnolia flowers is to show the angels where to find the peacocks if the colours in their feathers were to accidentally wash off in the rain.

Madelaine knows their haunting call, and that the beige and brown speckled ones are female. But, it is the male in all his splendour that enchants her. Her gaze travels from the delicate crown on his head, down his iridescent neck feathers, to his oh-so amazing tail that swoops back from his body to float mere inches above the ground like the cloak of a faery king in full majestic stride. And when those tail feathers shiver, spread open, and suddenly rise to stand up in a fan fit for a court of assembled queens, astonishment takes her breath away.

Tompie collects the tail feathers her peacock drops from time to time and keeps them in a slender glass vase in her living room. On that magical day Madelaine is about to return home when Tompie hands her five feathers and notices her puzzlement over how she will carry the feathers while riding her bike. Tompie tucks them into the back of Madelaine's shirt, plants a kiss on the top of her head, and waves her off to pedal home with five feathers fanning out from her shoulders.

On her way along the driveway, buoyed by all this love and beauty, she decides to give the feathers to her mother as a kind of bouquet to cheer her up. She leans her bike near the kitchen door, carefully draws the feathers from her shirt as one would extract arrows from a quiver, and goes in search of her mother.

She calls out and hears a faint response from the living room. With grand excitement, Madelaine bursts into the room proudly holding the gift of feathers aloft. She presents them to her mother, who is lying on the couch. Shock and horror freeze her mother's face; her eyes narrow, and pointing a finger towards the door, she orders in a cold, stern voice, "Get those dreadful things outside immediately! Don't ever bring them into the house again."

Madelaine turns and tiptoes from the room like a whipped puppy. All the way to her special thinking place she can hear her mother wailing and shouting for a servant to bring her ice for—Madelaine knows—her gin.

She crawls into the middle of her thinking place: a cluster of slender, smooth-barked trunks of a tree, in the centre of which there is space enough to hold one small girl and her peacock feathers. Madelaine lies down, places the feathers next to her, and looks up into the light dancing between the leaves and flowers. She tries to understand what she has done wrong and how to make it right, whatever it could be.

Eventually, an idea comes to her: leave four feathers in this kindly place where they will be safe. Take one feather to the laundry—a small building near the house—and wash away not only the iridescence, but also the magical eye-like marking that obviously holds no magic for her mother.

Madelaine scrubs the feather and rinses it again and again with no success. The colours remain. Zilli finds her feverishly working at the laundry sink and asks her what she is doing. In a torrent of teary words, Madelaine tells her.

Zilli cups Madelaine's chin in her palm, kindness welling from warm chocolate-coloured eyes, and explains that no amount of water and soap would ever remove the beauty the creator has given to the world, especially that of the peacock. "That is why," Zilli says, "that even when heaven's rains fall on the birds their beauty does not wash away."

Oh, so they roost in the magnolia tree not because their colours will wash off in the rain, but because that's just something peacocks do ... sometimes.

This explanation satisfies her. But still, Madelaine cannot shake off the intensity of her mother's cry of enraged pain. She carries the flayed, wet peacock feather to her thinking place and nestles it close to the others.

The fading image of the scrubbed feather brought Madelaine's awareness back to her mother's hospital bedside and compelled her to casually ask, "Mum, do you remember being angry with me over some peacock feathers I brought to you as a gift?"

Her mother massaged her bruised temples with her fingertips, clenched her jaw, and turned her eyes to the window.

Madelaine persisted. "What do peacock feathers mean to you, Mum?"

Madelaine waited for some time for a response, and was beginning to think she had pushed her mother too far, that she should simply leave her bedside and return to Brazil, when she heard *"Vanity and pride."*

"Vanity and pride?" Madelaine repeated, to be certain she had heard correctly.

Cords in her mother's neck tightened like ropes on a working winch. "Yes!" she hissed, and turned to face Madelaine with a ferocious look, cheeks suddenly flaming red.

"Peacocks signify pride and vanity. Good Christian values teach that pride and vanity are evil and will lead to all manner of wrong behaviour—especially for girls."

This spurted out as if she had held it inside for too long. The prominent flush drained from her face. Her eyes sank into a pool of helplessness.

Madelaine could barely absorb this outburst, although it was no less intense than it had been on that day long ago. Only now, as a woman, her view of her mother's shock and horror brought out an uncontrollable urge to soothe the bruise that had been inflicted on her sense of self—a bruise she continued to detect as she attempted to reach out to her mother.

Pushed to the brink of rude retaliation, Madelaine persisted. "It's the eyes that bother you, isn't it, Mum?"

"Oh, those eyes on the tail feathers," she moaned, her hands clenched into fists. She shivered with a spasm of revulsion. "Those eyes are the temptation we must avoid at all costs!"

As the word "costs" flew from her mouth, she flung her head back, thumped it against the pillows, and closed her eyes.

Madelaine, shocked by how much she wanted to shake her mother, withdrew to compose herself. She had no more questions to ask, nothing left to give her mother.

What can one do about a person who feels wronged and guilty to be alive?

She kissed her mother's sweaty forehead, stroked her mutilated arms, whispered that she would come back some other day, and left the recovery room.

Her dad was waiting in the hospital parking lot, smoking a cigarette in the shade of a jacaranda tree. He took one look at his daughter and said, "Let's head home, my girl."

She slid into the passenger seat. Emotions rose and surged like a stormy sea crashing onto the sand. She wept tears of sorrow and frustration about her inability to reach her mother.

Why is it so hard to let go of the belief that I am to blame for my mother's unhappiness?

Her Dad suggested she remember happier times.

"Like when?" She asked crossly, as if being angry would relieve her sense of shame and irretrievable love for her mother.

He reminded her of how efficiently her mother had run the household, and how she had overseen the gardens that were productive and beautiful in all seasons; how, when she was well she had been the life of the party, playing piano, and dancing. A wallflower she was not, and how lovely her singing voice had been.

These reminders, however, rather than soothing Madelaine, dredged up disloyal and unkind thoughts concerning her mother.

Without all of our faithful servants the household would not have run so efficiently; the gardens that provided us with flowers, fruits, and vegetables were maintained by a team of gardeners, and well, the parties ... jeez! I used to curl up at her feet under the piano when she was playing, so I would be close to her happiness, knowing that she would stay happy if unaware of me.

Their journey home from the hospital took hours, during which Madelaine decided to return to Rio de Janeiro sooner than planned. Her dad listened to her garbled, sob-laden admission about failing to understand why she felt responsible for her mother's illness, and her inability to be a dutiful daughter. He thoughtfully accepted her decision to return to Rio sooner than expected.

"Dad, am I an ungrateful daughter? Not the girl that Mum wanted me to be? A disappointment?"

He shook his head. "No, my girl. You are not an ingrate, nor a disappointment. In a fair world, a daughter cannot be blamed for her mother's 'inabilities.' I'm not sure what your mother wants from you, actually—or what she wants from life, except maybe to find her spirit and be able to rely on it. Neither you nor I can do that for her. Your whole life is ahead of you. Go ahead and live your life the best way you can." He lit a cigarette and blew smoke from the side of his mouth.

Madelaine sat still. With rapt attention, she waited for him to continue.

"I understand you feel there is nothing you can do here, but am glad you came. You always have cleaved your own path, and at times I worry that your passion for life and living could hurt you. Then I remember that you are strong enough to deal with whatever comes your way. Your spirit does not leave you. I'm certain, because I hold you in my heart and feel this—I always will, my girl."

She slid closer to his large, comforting frame and leaned her head on his shoulder. They travelled the remaining thirty miles in silence—a silence that continued as they entered the house and headed straight to his den. There, he poured each of them a large scotch whisky.

Later that night, numbed by single malt, exhausted from wading through longing to find love and compassion for her mother, and despite aching with sorrow over leaving her dad in a big empty house, Madelaine prepared for her return to Rio de Janeiro.

Soon after take off, the plane flew over the land of her birth. Her reflection in the window formed a frame across which, like an opening scroll, moved the view of an ochre blanket of earth decorated with patches of green, and flecked with violet shadows cast by scudding clouds.

Maybe duty is the social norm one adheres to when seeking approval from others ... Mum's internal battle must be overwhelming. No wonder she finds her spirit unreliable.

Madelaine, despite boarding school training, had not adhered to social norms from a young age; she had not accepted the demanding duties expected of a colonial daughter, and thus escaped the torment her mother experienced. Yes, escaping, as at this moment.

And then, as if the God of Expectation had one more salvo to hurl at her, Madelaine began chiding herself for not feeling guilty about what she could have done better in her life—specifically, during the visit to her mother in the hospital. She squirmed with discomfort, her senseless self-incrimination relentless, until realization struck: the very essence of duty makes a person feel ashamed for lacking what is expected by others.

Ahh. A way to release that damnable resolve.

Madelaine's rebel angels must have been listening, because this epiphany obliterated the encroaching shame, and awakened the desire to celebrate just as the flight attendant leaned towards her with a wine list.

Madelaine raised her glass to the future, her parents' ease of heart, her husband, the school she had opened for young children in Copacabana, and to all that Rio offered, the possibilities she had no idea existed until she had been swept up in a tide of unbridled sensuality and purpose.

DESTINATION: CANADA

1963

Their plan to drive north from Rio de Janeiro through the Americas became a real possibility one afternoon after Madelaine and Will taped together maps of all the countries in South, Central, and North America. Spread across the floor of their apartment, the completed collage resembled a carpet.

Madelaine knelt on Argentina to view the extent of the continents they would be travelling through. Will squatted over the Atlantic Ocean to get a westward view of the breadth of South America. They pinpointed capital cities in each country, made a list, and began the task of finding main routes that linked the cities. Their fingers travelled along lines that in some areas resembled cooked spaghetti that had been flung on the floor, curled tightly in some areas, and looping and wavelike in others. Rarely were roads marked as a straight line until they viewed the United States of America, where inland routes cut directly through the landscape. Returning to the South American portion of the map, they noticed that some roads dwindled and disappeared at the eastern spine of the Andes, re-emerged on the western side, meandered across a desert in Peru, and came to an end at the Pacific Ocean.

Their initial destination was San Francisco because Will had relatives living there, members of his family who had escaped from Poland and the Holocaust. But the US Embassy informed them that their places of birth—South Africa and Poland—restricted them from getting work permits for ten and twelve years, respectively. It was therefore necessary to find an alternative destination where restrictions for employment would not be as stringent.

The year was 1963. Madelaine and Will had fled the politics of South Africa in 1961 and moved to Rio de Janeiro. Will had a job as an architect and Madelaine opened a preschool. But the gradual breakdown of essential services such as the availability of milk, bread, and postage stamps, coupled with an inflation rate of one thousand percent, had spurred their plan to leave Brazil.

Since President Johnson had foiled their intended destination of San Francisco, they produced the carpet-like map collage that they now plotted over. Trailing along the road north from San Francisco, a few inches farther, their fingers stopped on Vancouver in the province of British Columbia.

"Hey! Here's a town on the coast ... uh, but wait. This is not the US. It's ... let's see ... Canada!"

"Canada? Oh, of course, that's where there's a different government. I mean, not the same as the US."

"Well, hell! That may work out for us. Let's go see them at their embassy and ask if Canada needs architects and preschool teachers."

"Let's also tell them we would like to live on the coast. The West Coast."

"If they are willing to give us visas and resident permits, we can live where we want!"

Madelaine and Will were welcomed at the Canadian embassy, told that yes, British Columbia needed architects and preschool teachers, and that they should return in three weeks to pick up entry visas and temporary resident permits.

The couple explained about their plan to drive a second-hand Volkswagen bus from Rio to Vancouver, and that they would most likely not be ready to depart from Rio in three weeks. The consul did not change his mind on hearing this, but his expression of bright and cheerful readiness to assist froze into open-mouthed disbelief and shock.

"Excuse me? You're doing what?"

"We'll be driving west from Rio, into Bolivia, across the Andes into Peru, and north from there."

"How long do you plan to take? When will you cross the Canadian border?"

"Uh, the drive could take four months. We'll give you the date of our departure from Rio as soon as we're ready to leave. Once that is determined, we will calculate the approximate date of our arrival at the US–Canada border. Would that be suitable?"

The consul nodded.

Applying for visas at the consulates and embassies representing the numerous countries they would be driving through turned out to be far less efficient than their visit to the Canadian embassy. Time and again, a note on an entry door informed visitors: "This office is closed. Return at another time."

In the Brazil of 1963, the only means of reaching those places to make an appointment was the telephone. Few homes had private telephones; most businesses had at least one. Voice mail and message machines were few and far between, so making an appointment with a consular official became increasingly frustrating when their calls were seldom answered. They soon learned to give up on the telephone and wait at closed doors for the duration of any given day, until somebody eventually came to work and agreed to attend to their inquiries.

It took three months before they had amassed visas, one by one. At the count of nine, when there were just two more to wait for, Madelaine discovered she was pregnant.

She was not about to change their patiently laid plans to drive to Vancouver simply because she was pregnant. Undaunted, they continued to collect supplies for the journey: canned and dehydrated food, a first-aid kit, and snakebite serum were crossed off the list. Friends even insisted they add weapons to their supplies—one each.

"What do we need weapons for?"

"You don't know about bandits in the hills? Murderers in the mountains?"

"But why would they want to kill us?"

"It's not about killing. It's about stealing your things. I've heard about bandits stealing windshield wipers, tires, and headlights to sell on the black market. I tell you, get some weapons! *Por favor*."[6]

So, Will bought a small pearl-handled revolver. Madelaine opted for a machete with a fine heft, a long, sharp blade, wooden handle, and leather sheath.

They left Rio on a spring day in August 1963, their van loaded with two tin trunks of canned and dehydrated food, their sleeping bags, mountain-climbing equipment, clothes, weapons, and a stack of official documents that included entry and resident permits for Canada. They headed in a north-westerly direction, towards Bolivia.

6   please (Portuguese)

A PIECE OF CAKE

It was mid-morning when Madelaine and Will pulled into a gas station in Santa Cruz, Bolivia, to fill up the tank and a jerry can. The mechanic struck up a conversation that opened with a question about their Guanabara State licence plates and continued with questions about where they were going.

"Cochabamba, via the mountain pass," explained Will.

The man blanched. "Señor! With respect, I must tell you maybe something you already know. This vehicle you drive," he gestured towards the van, "the engine … its power diminishes ten percent for every thousand feet higher you drive. Santa Cruz is one thousand. The summit where you're going is eleven thousand, and Cochabamba … Señor, it is eight thousand! Maybe your engine, it no will spark to start. *Si*?"

"Is there another road from here to there?"

"No, Señor. This is the only road."

They had read about the staggering elevations of the Andean mountain range, but nothing could have prepared them for the implacability of sheer rock walls, vertiginous drops into valleys deep enough to render the bottom invisible. Their determination to forge ahead kept them focused on the road even as the van sputtered in protest to the steady increase in elevation. Madelaine, unnerved by the sense of clinging to the lips of a foreboding mouth to avoid being swallowed, a mouth ready to engulf them in some dark hell, reminded herself to breathe and remain alert.

The stony dirt road, just wide enough for one-way traffic, had been cut into the side of one mountain after another. Bays (places for a vehicle to pull into) carved into rock walls were a short distance from each other. There were no guardrails to prevent vehicles from dropping into the abyss. Madelaine's qualms increased as night drew into the sky and their headlights barely penetrated the heavy darkness.

Once she had expressed her fears to Will, he agreed that it was suicidal to drive any farther, and pulled into a bay. They organized sleeping bags and checked the large copper bowl that travelled between them on the front seat, and which contained maps, identity documents, visas, cameras, and Will's revolver.

Then Madelaine climbed outside to stretch, and looked up. A narrow shred of sky, snagged, it seemed, on the jagged teeth of peaks miles above, was studded with millions of stars—stars that pulsed as if the sky was breathing. Suddenly, feeling as tiny as an ant, she scurried back into the familiar world of the van.

They heard no passing trucks or cars during the night. After a breakfast at dawn, Will tried to start the van. It would not start. He tried again, and again. Just as that spark the mechanic had mentioned caught, and the engine sputtered to life, they heard a truck approaching. It was too late to get ahead of the truck, so they watched it hurtle past.

The truck was fully loaded. Wooden planks had been added to increase the height of the sides, making room for people and livestock to travel above the goods that were being transported. It had no muffler and was moving at a speed of ear-popping volume. The load swayed; people clutched blankets wrapped around them; dust billowed, and stones flew.

Afraid the sputtering engine would die if they waited any longer, Will pulled out of the bay onto the road, the accelerator flat to the floor, encouraging a modest speed. All was well and good until they came around a bend and discovered the truck was directly ahead. Under no circumstances could they pass; nor could they slow down for fear of losing all engine power.

As the truck ahead had no rear-view mirrors, flashing the headlights was futile. Dust was pouring into the van and it was difficult to breathe; she could taste it. Will, his teeth bared, leaned over the steering wheel, growling and cursing, hoping a stone would not shatter their windshield. Madelaine, ready to explode with frustration, reached into the copper bowl and retrieved the revolver.

Will shot her a fiendish grin. "Fire over their heads, not at them!"

Madelaine removed the gun from its holster, released the safety catch and opened her window just enough to slide one arm out. She aimed over the abyss and fired. Echoes from the blast were barely receding when she fired again.

Will's shout of glee interrupted her inclination to blow across the opening of the barrel, as she had seen outlaws do in westerns.

"Hey, look! The truck is slowing down. Put the gun away. Yeah! He's pulling into that bay up ahead."

They chugged past the parked truck, chuckling at the driver who was checking his tires and oblivious to them. Before holstering Will's gun, Madelaine blew across the end of the barrel with great satisfaction.

"Ha! How do you like that, eh? A piece of cake."

Two hours later, they reached the summit at eleven thousand feet, relieved that the mechanic's dire prediction had not come to pass. They began their descent, careening down the road.[7] After negotiating yet another hairpin bend, Cochabamba suddenly came into view, nestled in a wide sunlit valley. Tilled fields were spread across hillsides like a quilt, undulating down towards a river that snaked around the outskirts of a small town.

The van sputtered and coughed to a stop as Will parked beneath one of the grand old willow trees that lined a town square. At the centre of the square, banks of flowers that surrounded an ornate fountain sparkled and quivered in the spray and splash of water. Across the square was a cathedral build by the conquistadores from hand-hewn blocks of stone. Scarlet and cobalt blue stained glass windows cast a softening glow onto the walls of this monument of worship.

Madelaine ran her tongue over dust-coated teeth. Not thinking of worship as much as the desire to lie down in the water cascading from the fountain, she tumbled out of her seat and leaned against the trunk of the tree. While shaking dust from her hair, she noticed the beribboned hem of a skirt and a sandaled foot on the other side of the tree trunk.

She peered around the trunk. A diminutive woman dressed in layers of wool shawls and a long skirt trimmed with brightly coloured ribbons was leaning against the tree. Two long braids of jet-black hair reached from her black bowler hat, down to her waist. Madelaine came farther around the tree and noticed that this tiny woman held a large wooden tray, which was supported by a broad strap that stretched across her upper back and shoulders. Laid out on the tray in precise rows were thick slices of orange

7   Yungas Road, the road they travelled from Santa Cruz to Cochabamba in 1963, is now known as Death Road. In 1995, the Inter-American Development Bank christened it as the "world's most dangerous road."

cake, which caused an instant rush of mouth-watering desire. The woman's perfectly round face, as bronze as an autumn moon, beamed up at Madelaine.

"A piece of cake?" she offered.

MADELAINE'S MACHETE

So far, a situation that required Madelaine to wield her machete had not arisen. Not exactly disappointed by this, she did wonder how effective she would be with it. Hopefully, unsheathing it and brandishing the sharpened blade at a threatening intruder would be sufficient.

Their van's limited power had turned out to be a blessing. The slow pace effectively acclimatized them as they ascended into the high Andean plains to Cuzco, the pre-Columbian capital of the Inca Empire.

They had learned that garage mechanics in most towns they passed through were reliable sources for news, advice on the state of the roads, access to shortcuts, and for knowing the distance between gas stations. The mechanic in Cuzco told them that transport trucks used the route they were embarking on as a shortcut through the mountains to the Pacific coast of Peru, and assured them this was the best way to cross the Andes in his part of the world.

This shortcut turned out to be a narrow, stony track of hairpin bends that wound upwards to the crest of a saddle-like formation of mountain rock and then dropped steeply into a deep, narrow valley, only to wind upwards again, and to drop again.

No wonder this road was unmarked on the maps we pored over in Rio. There were so many steep ascents and treacherous descents that Madelaine was set to imagining the shuddering halt of the earth's crust as it settled in a concertina-like fashion. Unerringly, it seemed, the Urubamba River, sacred to the Inca, coursed along through the valleys.

Somewhere along this road—around eighty miles from Cuzco—a shock absorber over the back right wheel collapsed. Now, with the back right sitting dangerously low, they nursed the van down yet another vertiginous drop. At a level area on a valley floor, Will pulled off the road and parked.

The Urubamba on the farther side of the road roared and tumbled over and around massive boulders with a sound so huge and insistent that Madelaine's ability to think was suspended.

She found an eddy that seemed safe to approach, rinsed her face, and filled the billycan with water to make tea. On a small fire of twigs encircled with river stones, she put the water on to boil. Meanwhile, Will jacked up the van and removed the wheel and shock absorber.

Over tea, they assessed the situation. They certainly could not travel back to Cuzco or continue forward in a van that was missing a shock absorber.

"The section on emergency repairs in the manual says that a shock absorber can be temporarily repaired by drilling a hole in the side of it, filling the thing with axle grease, and then closing the hole," said Will.

"Really? But we don't have axle grease or a drill, do we?"

"That is so. It looks like I have to get this bloody thing back to Cuzco, which means ..."

"Hitching a ride on a truck heading that way," finished Madelaine. "The mechanic in Cuzco said this was a truck route."

"But have we seen any trucks? No. And we can't leave the van with all our gear in it."

"I'll stay with the van. Really, I'll be fine. At any rate, I have my machete. Let's concentrate on a truck coming by. Maybe by sunset today we'll be lucky. Yes?"

With just two or three hours of daylight left—although for all she knew the mountains could rob this valley of light sooner—Madelaine went to collect firewood in preparation for a meal.

There was plenty of wood to be found. On her mission of gathering wood she noticed no evidence of human habitation and remarked on this discovery to Will.

"Well" he replied in a distracted way, the repair manual open on his lap, "that could mean we'll have no intruders bothering us—hey?"

She chopped vegetables bought at the market in Cuzco, tossed them into boiling water, and set up a place to eat. They sat on clean, dry ground covered with coarse sand that sparkled like quartz crystals.

A setting sun hovered on western mountain peaks. Millions of rainbows danced on the black rock wall across the Urubamba as rays of light met plumes of spray.

Rather than sitting on the side of the road to intercept a truck, they went to bed after dark, having made ready a bundle that consisted of the shock absorber, food, water, and vital identity documents. As usual, Will's revolver and Madelaine's machete were close at hand. Keeping in mind that the right rear end of the van was resting on a jack, they crawled into their sleeping bags carefully. She wondered if they would hear a truck engine over the roar of the river, but felt certain that at least headlights would wake them.

In the dead of night she awoke, not to the sound of an approaching truck or its headlights, but by the van rocking and shuddering. Lying still, all senses alert, voices of their friends in Rio surfaced in Madelaine's mind: "Bandits in the hills? Murderers in the mountains? They steal ..."

The van continued to rock, further encouraging images of thieves deftly taking anything they could, leaving the shell of a truck and one useless shock absorber.

Nudging Will, she whispered, "There's somebody outside."

"They'll leave," he murmured. "Just be quiet. Nothing we can do."

The rocking movement took on an incessant rhythm. Heart pounding, Madelaine pulled on a sweater and a pair of track pants, slithered from her sleeping bag, and unsheathed her machete. The full moon bathed the coarse white sand in milky light. Stars were so near and bright she was inclined to lower her head to pass under them.

Machete raised, she crouched and crept to the front of the van. Headlights, windshield wipers, and everything else appeared to be in its proper place, with no thief in sight. The van rocked again. Barely breathing, she snuck along the left side and around to the back.

A dark bulk was lurking under the fender near the jack that propped up the van. Brandishing her machete and ready to lunge, she paused at close range to assess her sanity. In that split second, Madelaine realized that this figure was not a thief after all. An enormous pig was using the fender to scratch its back.

The sow was facing the opposite direction. She grunted, moving her hips from side to side, her teats swinging. Madelaine would have liked to observe the sow's pleasure a while longer, but she needed to move her away from that precarious back end. How was she to do that without hurting the sow, or endangering herself?

Without giving it another thought, she swung the machete as if playing forehand in a tennis game, whacking the sow's rear end with the flat of her weapon. The sow jerked away from the fender, causing a dangerous wobble of the van.

Feeling quite relieved, Madelaine sheathed her machete, watched the sow trot away, crawled into her sleeping bag, and asked the stars to send a truck in the morning.

Soon after daybreak they heard a truck engine gear down, and suddenly there it was, coming around the bend. They stood on the roadside and waved. With squealing brakes and grinding gears, the fully loaded truck stopped a good distance away. Will, carrying his bundle of supplies, ran to the truck, exchanged words with the driver leaning out the window, and a minute later climbed up onto the back of the truck as it began to move. *That guy is in a hurry*, thought Madelaine, watching the truck until it disappeared around a bend.

By nightfall Will had not returned. Lulled to sleep by the sound of the Urubamba, and with her machete close by, Madelaine slept undisturbed until a tender pre-dawn flush of pink in the sky drew her into the day. A mug of hot sweet tea warming her hands, she became mesmerized by the tendrils of smoke rising from her small, fire-like messages from ancient times.

Sunlight crept over the rims of mountain peaks; its beams struck the quartz sand, bathing her in clear, sparkling daylight. Engrossed in these moments of beauty, she did not hear the truck until it came into view. It slowed. The passenger door flew open and out leapt Will. The engine revved and the truck clambered past on its way to the mountain pass they would negotiate later that day.

"All's well?" inquired Will, sipping his tea. "No intruders? The sow didn't return?"

"All's well, thanks. And you? Where did you sleep last night?"

"In the house of the mechanic and his family—they live next to the garage. It was good because I didn't have far to go when the shock was repaired late last night." Impatient to get going, Will walked to the van. "Let's get this thing on the road now. How about I replace it and the wheel while you douse the fire and pack up. Good?"

With the shock absorber temporarily repaired and installed and the back wheel securely in place, the long, slow, and extremely steep ascent to the summit of the mountain pass began. Eventually, they would get to the western side of the Andes in Peru.

A COLOMBIAN COBBLER

It is early morning on the coast of Colombia. Mist lingers over the Pacific Ocean, and small waves break and hiss across tawny sand. Leaning against their van, Will and Madelaine sip tea from tin mugs and wait for the sun to rise while taking in the surroundings. Behind them is a scattering of small buildings arranged on three sides of a village square. The fourth side of the square is open to the beach.

At the water's edge small wooden fishing boats emerge through the dawn mist. One by one, each boat carried on the crest of a wave careens onto the sandy shore. Voices fill the air; fishermen leap from their boats into the shallows and drag them farther ashore.

People are arriving in dust-laden trucks and donkey-drawn carts loaded with a wide variety of goods. Once parked in the square a frenzy of unloading begins. Marketers set up stalls, lay out their wares, tether donkeys, and blow life into embers contained in tin drums, where tasty food will be cooked throughout the day.

Will and Madelaine's journey from Brazil through Bolivia, Peru, and Ecuador has brought them into Colombia. Madelaine's pregnancy has also undeniably progressed. Aside from a protruding belly and a constant craving for fresh vegetables, her feet are no longer comfortable in flip-flops. She desperately hopes to find a sturdy pair of sandals at the market.

They buy fish, vegetables, fruit, and bread. She is thinking of carrying her full basket back to the van when, much to her delight, she sees a cobbler setting up shop under a tree at the side of the square.

The cobbler understands what she needs, and while he selects two rectangular shapes cut from car tires, she sits on a wooden box. With quiet efficiency, he asks her to place a bare foot on each piece of car tire. He outlines her feet with a chunk of chalk and invites her to return to her seat on the box.

With a lethal-looking blade, he shapes each rectangle to that of the outline of her feet by deftly paring away the excess rubber and discarding the outer edges. Satisfied with what he has fashioned, he nails pre-made leather straps onto each piece of car tire that is now the shape of the sole of her foot.

Madelaine's sandals are ready. With a flourish, he hands them to her to try on. They are perfectly comfortable. She pays him the equivalent of two dollars and walks away, with a new spring in her steps cushioned on an inch of rubber. Little did she know that day of how long she and her sandals would accompany each other over time.

DEAD WOMAN SMOKING

1963–1964

According to myth, Central America was created in the shape of a caiman crocodile, and by the way volcanoes are indicated by red triangles on the map, it is not difficult to imagine they are scales on the spine of such a beast. Will and Madelaine are driving towards San José, the capital of Costa Rica, a country that boasts one hundred and twelve volcanoes, seven of which are active.

The landscape is flat and carpet-like, the scenery lush and green. Steep-sided hills in the distance rise into dense clouds. Treed gullies criss-cross cultivated valley floors. Trails of mist waft across the road, intermittently interrupting their view as if they are driving through loosely woven strands of light.

It is December 27, 1963. After more than four months, Will and Madelaine are almost halfway between Rio de Janeiro and their destination of Vancouver, Canada. By her reckoning, her pregnancy is about halfway along, too. The estimated time of arrival at the US–Canada border, which they had told the

Canadian consulate in Rio de Janeiro before their departure, was clearly not accurate. They are already overdue.

Before their departure from Rio, rather than taking all their funds for the journey with them, they made arrangements with Will's father to send funds to various stops along the way via Western Union. This plan worked reasonably well in large towns where a Western Union waited to serve them.

They expected the same in San José. The plan was to go to Western Union, pick up the cheque, cash it at the bank, replenish their food cache, and fill the gas tank. The gas gauge was teetering dangerously close to "E."

It is mid-afternoon when they approach the town of San José and are suddenly engulfed in fog. The centre of town is in darkness. Streetlights cast no beams. They are merely suspended in a dense fog—except that this fog is falling like rain, accumulating on sidewalks and in drains, rippling and shifting on the street like black snow. Pedestrians walk gingerly, their heads and faces wrapped in cloth. Some wear masks.

Will turns down a street that leads to the Western Union office. Once parked, they step outside into air that is thick with showering ash. They run to the building and duck inside.

The man behind the counter is welcoming. He listens attentively to their request to pick up a cablegram of money, nods, and calls for someone to retrieve the cablegram addressed to Will. While they wait, Madelaine asks him about the ash in the air.

"That is Irazu," he informs her in a nervous whisper, as if voicing the name could evoke a dark entity.

Upon hearing the name, Madelaine recalls an ancient legend about an active volcano, Irazu, which was the only female; the remaining six active volcanoes were male.

"*Dios, M⁸adre Mia*," he says and makes the sign of a cross. His voice rises with a combination of pride and superstition. "Irazu is volcano near our city, San José. She is the highest of all mountains in our country."

Madelaine visualizes the red triangle on the map that indicates Irazu and nods to encourage him to continue. Instead of telling her more about Irazu, he launches into another story; his story of President Kennedy's visit to San José in March 1963.

"He have big car. Drive by all our people in the streets. We wave flags of our country, flags of Estados Unidos. We make big welcome. He give money for new houses. Everybody say '*Gracias,* thank you Señor President Kennedy,' and then he go away. Before the day is finished, Irazu cough big smoke, big ash. Every day, Irazu smoke and cough, cough and smoke. Ash breaks houses— it is heavy—and now food is under the ash; there is no grass for animals."

A machine clatters behind him and he turns his attention to that. Madelaine is interested in how this man links Kennedy's visit with Irazu, and asks if he knows of the legend that tells why Irazu is a female volcano and the others are male.

He nods. His voice drops to a whisper as he leans towards her over the counter, as if drawing her into a conspiracy.

"Why, yes! Is true. Irazu is woman. You see, in ancient time an important leader and his people owned all the rich valleys around here. This leader had a most beautiful daughter, Irazu. His favourite child. Another leader come and make war to get the rich valleys. The father of Irazu, he go to the gods of the highest mountain and he sacrifice this daughter. To please the gods, to let him win. *Ay!* The battle, it was fierce, and the father, he was losing. So, he calls to the spirit of Irazu for help. Immediately, that highest mountain

8   God, Mother Mine - Spanish

sends smoke, ash, and rocks onto the enemy. They are destroyed. Yes, Irazu, she heard her father."

Without drawing another breath, he returns to his story of Kennedy's visit to San José.

"Some of our people, they say President Kennedy is good, but his money, it is no good for us. Maybe the gods of the volcanoes, they tell Irazu to tell us this? Maybe they are dissatisfied? God forgive me, but now I ask to what or where does a person pray, Señora?"

"It is a deep question, Señor. May heaven hear your prayers, and the volcano gods your plea."

As if Madelaine's question was the best thing to happen to him that day, aside from someone to whom he could relate his Irazu/Kennedy story, he gladly gave directions to the soccer field downwind from Irazu, where he believed they would be safe and hopefully sleep well—which was especially important for the soon-to-be Mama.

Early the next morning an incessant tapping pulls Madelaine from a deep sleep. Her first thought is that the ash from Irazu has turned into pebbles. She worries about the windows of the van. Then she hears a voice urging them to wake up and receive the money order from Western Union.

Sure enough, a messenger from Western Union is waiting by the van. His gas mask is pushed up to his forehead. Smiling triumphantly, he hands Will an envelope containing a message that two hundred dollars is waiting for him at Banco Americano.

The messenger hops onto his bicycle, lowers his gas mask, and peddles away. Madelaine watches him disappear across the field, then looks to the east with the hopes of seeing the sun rise. Alas— the sky is the colour of bruised apricots, streaked with steel-grey clouds tinged a lurid orange. It seems to be glowering with menace.

They drive into town to Banco Americano. With scarves wrapped around their heads and across their faces, Will and Madelaine shuffle through the black snow eagerly, only to find the doors of the bank locked. A sheet of paper flutters from a nail on the door. Holding it still with both hands, Will reads the notice out loud.

"The bank will be closed from December 28, 1963 to January 2, 1964, for the holidays. We apologize for any inconvenience. Happy New Year."

Now what? Weighed down with a sense of defeat as gloomy as the world outside, feeling thwarted and helpless in a city of people struggling with a very real threat to their health and livelihoods, Will and Madelaine muster what imaginative reserves remain and begin devising ways to survive six days with no gas and a meagre supply of food. The decision to find a consulate or an embassy before they also close for the holidays, to ask for a temporary loan until the bank opens, galvanizes them both to locate the British Embassy on a city map. Both Will and Madelaine have South African passports. Certainly, with South Africa once having been a British colony, that would be in their favour.

Hoping the gas gauge is not entirely accurate, they head for the British Embassy. While stopped at a red light, Madelaine notices the unmistakable Union Jack prominently displayed on the rear fender of a car in the lane to her right. What further encourages them is the "DC" on the licence plate: diplomatic corps.

They follow the car, which leads them directly to the office of the British Consulate.

A grey-haired man wearing a crumpled, white linen suit alights from the car they followed and walks briskly towards the building. He has not noticed Will and Madelaine, so she calls out to him.

He stops and turns around. Will and Madelaine introduce themselves and explain their plight, matching his stride as he resumes his hurried pace to the building and into an office. They follow him.

"Hmm … money, is it?"

"Yes sir, it is money we need. Until the banks open on January 2."

"I see. Give me your passport, my dear, in exchange for ten dollars."

Madelaine promptly hands him her passport and receives ten dollars from his wallet.

"There we are, then. Must be off now. See you in the New Year."

He returns his wallet to his pocket and places Madelaine's passport in a drawer, which he locks. Picking up a bundle of mail and shooing them out, he adds, "Head for the hills, my dear. That way." He flings his arm in an easterly direction. "This ash does a body no good. Cheerio!"

They carefully apportion the money to cover food, mostly canned—Irazu's ash has taken its toll on vegetable gardens. They buy gas, fill water bottles, and head for the hills as advised.

The road is narrow and winds around hairpin bends. It takes them to increasingly higher elevations until, quite suddenly, they arrive at a cairn of stones, which marks the summit and the end of the road. From where Madelaine stands at the cairn, the mountain falls away—bare earth peppered with boulders—into a deep, dark valley shrouded in mist. To her right is a meadow of lush green grass sprinkled with white daisies. Will parks on the edge of this flower-strewn meadow, near a cluster of smooth-barked laurel trees and a calm stream of crystal-clear water. The sun is shining, and the air is clean. They agree that this is the perfect place to wait out the holidays.

During the night, Madelaine wakes to a heavy rain drumming on the roof of the van. By morning, the rain has not let up, so they remain cocooned in their sleeping bags. The windows become steamy. Trees are dark smudges in an opaque, wet world. The stream gurgles and gushes with renewed intensity.

Four days pass, each one like the last. Madelaine is close to cursing the volcano gods when she awakes to silence and utter stillness. The drumming rain has stopped. She opens the door, looks up at the sky expecting to see a break in the cloud cover, and is elated when she is greeted by a milky moon against a blanket of sparkling stars.

New Year's Day, January 1, 1964, dawns amidst fingers of sunlight that push through a swirling mist, nudging Will and Madeleine to stir from torpor. They decide to wait until the sun's rays have warmed the air before venturing from their cozy cocoons.

A few minutes later, the sound of a car engine straining to climb the steep incline towards the summit piques their curiosity. Neither wants to talk to anybody, especially strangers appearing through the mist. They agree to ignore whoever it is and remain in their sleeping bags, stone-faced and still.

The car stops a short distance away from the van. While staring up from her sleeping bag at steamy windows, Madelaine imagines that somebody steps from the car, perhaps to stretch and look around. She hears two car doors slam shut. *They must notice the van.* She groans and lights a cigarette.

The sound of shoes sloshing through the sticky sodden grass stops outside the van. Two shadowy figures peer through a foggy window, hands cupped around their eyes. Two men. They each wipe a peephole on the steamy window and peer through.

They step back, shaking their heads. One scratches the back of his head and turns away, kicks the stones of the fire pit, and wanders off out of Madelaine and Will's view, only to quickly return to his companion who is staring at the ground.

Madelaine and Will sit absolutely still, Madelaine holding a smoking cigarette, observing this pair of perplexed men as they walk away. A few paces from the van, one of the men grabs at his companion's arm and with loud urgency declares, "Well, they are two in there, and they are dead, that's for sure."

The second man shouts in alarm. "They are not dead, as you say. One is smoking!"

Madelaine peers through their peephole and watches them struggle to move faster than the wet ground will allow, arms flailing to keep their balance, expletives peppering the stillness. They leap into the car, slamming the doors as they speed away, engine revving.

Imagining the two hurtling down the mountain, arguing over whether the bodies in the van were dead or alive has Will and Madelaine enjoying a good laugh—the first laugh in days, which finally moves them from their cocooned existences into warm sunlight.

The following day, transactions at the bank are complete, their food cache is replenished, the tank is full of gas, and the British Consulate is duly paid back in return for Madelaine's passport. Determined, Will drives from San José in a northerly direction.

Engaging the windshield wipers to clear away Irazu's ashes yet again, Will clears his throat. "You know, I'm starting to believe that Irazu really is a female volcano, 'cause she's certainly a force to be reckoned with."

"I hear no complaints from all those male volcanoes," said Madelaine.

He winks at her. They each toss a salute toward the ash-laden clouds, and Madelaine feels fortunate to be escaping the wrath of Irazu.[9]

9   Irazu's ash continued to fall on San José and
     surrounding areas for two years.

SANDALS AND SONS

1964

Three months later, their van sputtered through no-man's land to the Peace Arch crossing at the Canadian border. They had travelled nineteen thousand miles from Rio de Janeiro through eleven countries. The fact that they had actually reached their destination had not quite registered in their minds at this point. Will was waved into a parking spot by a border guard who eyed them and their licence plate with undisguised curiosity. Madelaine considered what a person in uniform might make of their appearance. *Here he is, guarding this clean and tidy border, when a very strange couple seeks to cross: a bearded, shaggy-haired man accompanied by a woman in track pants and a voluminous shirt billowing over a protruding belly, her tire-soled sandals on calloused feet emerging from a dusty, dented vehicle with unrecognizable licence plates.* She sighed nervously.

The guard craned his neck like an inquisitive gopher when Madelaine eased her very pregnant body out of the parked van. Carrying a stack of documents already organized for this crossing into Canada, they entered the Canada Customs and Immigration building and walked up to the counter. Madelaine was struck by the orderly calmness in the large office area where she and Will now stood. The man behind the counter greeted them courteously, which was a pleasant change from how they had been treated at many of the borders they had already crossed.

The man examined their passports and was about to inspect the remaining documents when he paused. "Hey, Fred," he called across the room. "Guess what? They're here! They made it!"

"Who's here?" came a voice from behind a cubicle.

"That couple. The ones driving from Brazil."

"You're kidding!"

Fred emerged from his cubicle smiling broadly. He approached the counter, glanced at their passports, and then extended his hand to shake Will's and then Madelaine's.

"Welcome to Canada. Wow! You're, let's see … four months late. But you're here." He glanced at Madelaine's belly. "Congratulations. Please, take a seat while we verify your documents."

By the time their documents had passed inspection, Madelaine had been given a cup of tea and a chocolate digestive biscuit. She reassured Fred who was concerned about her advanced state of pregnancy that they had a family friend who would help her find a doctor and a hospital in which to give birth. Will was required to hand over his revolver for firearms inspection, and to leave it with customs until they cleared it. Madelaine's machete was of no interest to them.

The feeling of excitement and relief to have finally made it to Canada began to seep into their previous sense of unreality. They were also somewhat nervous. They had been on the road for eight months and the baby was due in five weeks, which left them little time to find an apartment, meet with a doctor, and collect clothes and bedding for their baby.

As Will navigated through traffic, Madelaine searched for the mountains she had read about, but they were obscured by heavy, grey banks of clouds. The cold and rainy weather would not be easy to adjust to. This was only one aspect of what she gradually began to understand as a form of culture shock. From which culture she was adjusting, she was not certain.

The doctor with whom she had made an appointment was congenial and polite—until he asked for proof of her pregnancy. Madelaine, who felt she looked like a whale, was astounded that he wanted proof.

"I'm sorry, doctor. Have you just asked me for proof of my pregnancy? I think it's obvious, isn't it?"

"Yes, I can see you are pregnant, but I require documentation from your previous doctor. Do you have that?"

"No, I don't."

"Surely, you must have been attended to by a physician, to verify your condition, no?"

"I did not need anyone to verify my pregnancy. I simply knew. And in any case, if there had been a physician, he would be in Rio de Janeiro."

He raised an eyebrow. "Where?"

"My husband and I have driven from Rio de Janeiro to Vancouver. I need to find a physician to attend the birth of our baby."

"I am sorry. I cannot do that without the paperwork."

Madelaine heaved her heavy body out of the chair, waddled to the door, opened it, and stepped from his office. *What the hell was that all about? Bloody paperwork! I'm pregnant, not sick!*

"Ah, excuse me! Wait a minute." The doctor called after her. "Where did you say you came from?"

"Brazil. By road."

"Hmm ... That's what I thought I heard. Please, take a seat. I will see what we can do for you."

Madelaine, feeling numb to any further emotional jerks, sat down again and looked directly into the doctor's eyes. "Please be certain you will perform the task, doctor. I would not like to waste your time. Or mine."

Five weeks later, Will and Madelaine's first child is ready to be born. Madelaine hurriedly packs a small bag, realizing that she does not own bedroom slippers. She tosses her tire-soled sandals into her bag. Will drives her to the hospital.

Her doctor is at the hospital when they arrive. She is placed in a ward of sixteen beds, all occupied by women like herself who are immigrants from other lands, other cultures.

Thirty hours of intermittent contractions and seeping amniotic fluid brings on desperation for attention. Madelaine has been ignored for too long. Mannered civility be damned, she bangs on the metal locker at her bedside, shouts for a nurse, and waits. Nothing. She throws a glass tumbler into one of the porcelain sinks. It shatters with a satisfying crash.

This brings not one, but two nurses into the ward, pushing a gurney. They ask her to climb onto it and place her bathrobe and sandals at her feet. With welcome efficiency, she is wheeled into the labour room and rolled onto a bed. A nurse prepares a vein in her arm into which they plug an induction drip. She is covered with a sheet, told to lie on her side, and to breathe deeply.

Her sandals that have carried her many miles are neatly placed side by side on the floor next to the bed, an arm's length away. Within minutes, her body begins to respond to the induction drip, which brings on increasingly intense contractions. Mother and child are a single unit of effort. Deep, steady breathing. Concentration and focus curl inward, reaching to touch this life within her, encouraging its passage into the light.

The rattle of a metal trolley intrudes on the increasing depth of her inward journey. She senses someone approaching from behind. With no introduction, or warning, the sheet is quickly pulled aside. Her inward process comes to a halt as she hears the snap of surgical gloves. Fingers probe her innards.

Refusing to even consider bringing civility to this moment, this invasive interruption, she reaches for a sandal and whacks this person's arm.

"Get out of here!" she snarls.

He roughly withdraws his fingers and rushes to the door. The sandal sails through the air after him, missing his head by a few inches. It lands in the corridor outside.

Madelaine is trying to settle back into the process of connecting with her baby when a fast-moving, broadly built woman strides in, the sandal held aloft, demanding to know if Madelaine was a claymore-wielding Celt or some Sassenach fool from yonder climes.

"I am a Celt from Africa in need of help with this birthing."

The midwife drops the offending sandal close to its mate and swings into action. Imperious, brooking no interruptions, she inspires confidence by arranging Madelaine in a comfortable position and wheels her to a delivery room into the care of her doctor. At first light the following morning Madelaine and Will's son is born, and a few days later she brings him into their new home in Vancouver. Madelaine thrives on making a home and on mothering, as if it were second nature. Mother and son explore the neighbourhood, often stopping on a sandy beach where, concealed under a sarong, she breastfeeds him to the sound of waves lapping the shore. She is glad to be settled into an apartment, and does not miss the nomadic lifestyle she and Will had accustomed themselves to while on the road north. They have made good friends, and a sense of camaraderie and stability infuse their lives.

When Madelaine becomes pregnant for the second time—
twenty-one months after the birth of their first son—she returns to
that first doctor. After exchanging a pleasant laugh over their very
first meeting, he promises attentive monitoring and she enrols in a
prenatal class. Madelaine has a clearer idea of what to expect with
this birth, except that she still does not own bedroom slippers.

She packs basic necessities in a small bag, and once again,
tosses in her tire-soled sandals. A friend keeps their first-born
company at home while Will drives her to the hospital.

With the preliminaries taken care of, she is wheeled down a
corridor on a gurney and left to wait outside the delivery room,
her bathrobe and sandals lying at her feet.

Through the layered sounds of crying infants, phones ringing
in the distance, and her own grunting sighs, she hears familiar,
determined footsteps. Madelaine opens her eyes and peers
through the curtain of dishevelled hair that's fallen across her face.
The midwife is approaching with a group of students in tow.

They arrive at the foot of Madelaine's gurney, and the students
shuffle to a standstill around the midwife. She reaches towards
the sandals, pauses, and then gently moves the hair away from
Madelaine's face. Recognition brings a warm, welcoming smile to
an otherwise stern face.

"Och! Lassie," she says, her hand resting gently on Madelaine's
forehead. She turns to her students. "This one? A wild one, I tell
ye. Crossed the Americas carrying her first bairn, and ye better be
knowing that these are nae ordinary sandals. They've been known
to fly through the air! Och, Lassie. Here ye are agin!"

MOTHER TONGUE

1970s

❝ I'd like to meet the Indigenous people of this part of the world. Where would I find them?" Madelaine asked a man sitting across from her at a table laden with a traditional Christmas turkey and all the trimmings. Having immigrated to Canada a few months prior to this evening of feast and festivity, she and her husband Will did not know many people in Vancouver. They were pleased to have been invited to join a group of four married couples. It was 1964.

Having grown up in South Africa, surrounded and cared for by Indigenous people, Madelaine had incorrectly assumed that Indigenous people everywhere in the world were somehow engaged in the lives of settlers from Europe—albeit as slaves.

She waited patiently for a reply, while observing how he ate. Thin lips barely touched the food he put in his mouth, and he chewed with his front teeth like a rat. He mopped his pink, sweaty forehead with a napkin before replying, "You won't see many of those people around here … in the civilized world."

"Oh? Why not?"

"We moved them onto reservations, far away. Let's see … this was some decades ago."

"May I ask who you mean by 'we'?"

He laid down his knife and fork, swallowed a mouthful of turkey, and speaking through his nose as if it were necessary to patronize her ignorance said, "I work for the Canadian government in the department of Indian Affairs. You, as a new immigrant to Canada, probably don't realize the dedication and commitment required to *control* the savages. That is what Indigenous people are: savages."

"But, aren't we all immigrants—or should I say, settlers—new or not? I mean the Indigenous people are not immigrants …"

With a voice rising in increased tones of disbelief because of her interruption, or possibly because he perceived her as ignorant, he went on. "They live through their communication with nature! Doesn't that tell you how backward they are? And, despite efforts of the church and government to civilize them, they do not comply."

Madelaine was torn between feeling sorry for the man's frustration and a bile-inducing flash of rage at his unapologetic racism. The mention of Indian Affairs brought to mind an image from her childhood of a beefy, red-faced man extolling innumerable advantages of separating the South African population into groups based on skin colour. She recalls that man's obvious pride in his position in South African Bantu Affairs as he laid out the Nationalist Party's plans to create apartheid laws to control "the blacks."

The Nationalist Party won the 1948 election—and the world knows where that took South Africa's Indigenous people and their "masters." Madelaine experienced extreme discomfort in 1948, and now this man across the table had dredged up more uneasiness.

Certain she would unleash a socially unacceptable tirade, she turned her attention to others at the table without responding.

The feeling of having been smeared stayed with her, though, as if a greasy hand had swiped across her rear-view mirror.

While on her way to the kitchen with an armload of dirty plates, Madelaine tried again, asking his wife where she would find the Indigenous people of British Columbia.

"Don't bother," she hissed through lips caked with scarlet lipstick, pushing Madelaine aside to reach the kitchen counter.

"But why on earth should I not?"

"Indigenous people who are still alive are far from here—on reservations. This is a big province, y'know. Besides, smallpox killed most of them, anyway." She rinsed her hands as she spoke, scrubbing nails painted blood red as if to say, "Get this filth off me!"

Oh.

Although the red-nailed woman and her husband's views were Madelaine's first encounter of racism in Canada, they weren't the last. She continued to collide with an increasing number of people who held similar beliefs. Many even became angry with Madelaine for asking about Indigenous people. She was accused of being a white woman from South Africa where she and "her kind" were evidently unsuccessful at controlling "the blacks." It was as if her skin colour precluded her from the right to locate the Indigenous people of British Columbia—of Canada, actually.

Although stung by the acrimony she encountered, this fuelled determination. Madelaine's search continued for almost a decade, until she applied for the position of workshop facilitator, to support an organized group of Indigenous women planning to set up community preschools.

Violet was one of a group of elders who interviewed her for the position. In a straightforward manner that Madelaine grew to trust and enjoy over time, she asked, "So, what is your mother tongue? English?"

"isiZulu."

After puzzled looks were passed from one elder to another, Madelaine quickly explained.

"I was born in South Africa to Scottish and Irish parents who were colonial landowners. For the first five years of my life, the Zulu people, who worked for my parents, raised me in their language, and imprinted me with their humanity. I am eternally grateful for that."

Madelaine was not entirely certain whether her explanation was responsible, but the panel of elders agreed to hire her. She went on to conduct training workshops for women from Vancouver Island communities who were eager to set up daycare centres and preschools for their young children.

The workshops were conducted in the conference room of a centrally located motel where Madelaine was accommodated.

Inspired by the participation of women who signed up for the training, Madelaine was drawn into their collective spirit of sheer determination to forge forward, as exemplified by a dynamic ability to cooperate and a hearty sense of humour. She also felt as if she had finally stepped onto solid ground and discovered a familiarity of spirit.

During one of their discussion periods, a grandmother heaved herself out of her chair asking to be heard, and in a voice resonant with passion stated that, "Nobody, however hard they try, can kill the roots of a mother tongue unless they kill the person. The invaders tried, we all know that. They took the young from their families and forced them into residential schools where they were severely punished for speaking their mother tongue. The invaders tried many ways to break us and ruin our sacred ways. Many of our people died because of that. Those who survived the cruelties— some of us are here in this room—know that by bringing our language to life again, we sustain traditional conversation. Through and with our young children we will nourish our roots."

That grandmother's covenant about the root of a tongue—a mother tongue, no less—lit a flame within Madelaine. She recalled her Zulu nanny saying, "Ai, child of ours, the root of your tongue comes straight from your young heart. This way you will grow true and strong."

Towards the end of the first phase of the workshop series, Violet invited Madelaine to attend a longhouse ceremony. She warmed to this gesture of generosity, but most of all, she felt accepted and befriended.

"Dress warm," Violet instructed. "Go to that bridge by your motel. We'll pick you up before dark."

Cottonwood trees lined the riverbanks, their golden yellow leaves slapping against each other in the evening breeze, in concert with the rushing sound of the river. Overhead, steel-grey clouds threatened rain, while a clear band of western sky held the setting sun in a moment of brilliance that lit up the lower edge of the blanket of cloud. Sunbeams burst in-between tree trunks, alighting on the bridge and Madelaine's lone figure, waiting.

After the sun disappeared, cold air whipped at her cheeks. Madelaine was glad she had heeded Violet's instruction to dress in layers: a wool shirt, sweater, scarf, black calf-length coat, thick socks, and rugged boots.

Like a foreign entity, darkness encroached silently, enveloping her. Madelaine knew that it was essential she stayed put until Violet's van arrived. To quell fears that Violet had forgotten, and to accept the dense darkness of a wintry night, she practiced a song learned from the women, putting Zulu words to it—words that evoked the protection of night spirits.

Madelaine beat a rhythm on the steel railing of the bridge, and danced and sang. She was so engrossed that only when headlights illuminated the trees and the bridge did she hear, "Hey! You wild woman! Get in here."

They drove along a road that meandered through tall trees, across a bumpy field, and towards an impressively large rectangular log structure. Entrance doors to the longhouse were splayed open, revealing a scene of people moving about, laughing, and talking. A blazing fire stoked with logs longer than the height of a tall man sent sparks flying through a smoke hole in the roof.

Once inside, Violet seated Madelaine in-between two people on one of the bleachers and promised to return. In a horseshoe formation at the far end of the longhouse, seven structures the size of clothes closets were covered with blankets, animal hides, and sacks.

The longhouse was filled to capacity. Citrus scents from shared bags of mandarin oranges mingled with those of wood smoke and warm bodies. Steady drumbeats kindled greetings, conversations, and bursts of laughter that seemed to billow in waves of triumphant joy.

Suddenly, a piercing howl tore through the immense space. Drumbeats ceased. Fires hissed and crackled. A figure emerged from one of the closet-like structures. Madelaine looked questioningly at Violet.

"Watch and listen. This is a young warrior. I'll explain later."

Concealed by a costume fashioned from field grass, he moved forward a few paces and then dropped into a crouch. The grasses hissed as if caught in a breeze, settling back into place with a shushing sound.

Slowly, he rose and stood motionless. Two guides stepped forward and steered him away from the fire. Yipping like a wolf pup, consumed by an energy force known only to him, he danced. The costume swayed like field grass in a late summer wind. His howls soared to the rafters and burst into song as his arms, bent at the elbows, reached through the shield of grass. His palms faced upward, in a gesture of greeting that to Madelaine seemed to also carry a sense of gratitude and acceptance of the power of life.

Guides removed the costume to reveal a young adult male dressed in a deer hide breechclout. He stood with his head held high, heaving chest glistening with sweat. Then, in a sacred spiritual gesture for which Violet respectfully denied explanation, the guides draped a blanket over his shoulders, covering him once again. Adorned with this ceremonial blanket, he approached the group of elders. They rose to receive him. The young warrior moved from one elder to the next, acknowledged by each one before he was offered a seat. The elders resumed their respective seats on the bench after the warrior was settled.

Throughout the night, one by one a young warrior emerged from his closet-sized enclosure at the far end of the longhouse, to dance alone and sing his spirit song, wearing a unique, concealing costume. One danced in a cloak made of feathers, another in a costume that resembled strips torn from a cassock, and still another wore strips of cedar bark that had been woven into a basket-like shroud.

The purpose of the gathering, she later learned from Violet on the way to the motel at dawn, was to welcome initiates who had been on a four-month vision quest—solo.

Four months? That night on the bridge, I had fretted after barely an hour! Then again, I had voiced a song in my mother tongue, beat a rhythm, and danced over the Cowichan River.

Madelaine returned to her home in Vancouver after accepting Violet's invitation to attend a celebratory feast in four weeks to honour the warriors. Violet drew a map of the route Madelaine would take from the Victoria ferry terminal to the longhouse celebration.

"Get there before dark and bring a flashlight—they have no electricity. Oh, you could be put to work in the kitchen. You okay with that?"

"Absolutely!

Violet's map led Madelaine along a dirt road to the fringe of an old-growth forest, and that was it. Why had she not noticed this dead end on the map?

Madelaine got out of her car and walked alongside the fringe of the forest searching for tire tracks. She stretched her hearing beyond the enormous and enveloping silence for any clue that would lead her in the right direction. Then she caught the scent of wood smoke and, wafting through that, the aroma of food cooking. Salmon. She hurried back to her car and departed from this seemingly sacred site that was guarded by a wall of giant evergreen trees.

Retracing the route that had led her to the forest's edge, she came upon a stand of alders and evidence of a tire-worn track that wound through the trees. Amazed at having missed it, but certain that this new direction was correct, she continued driving, following the increasingly potent aromas of food and wood smoke.

A massive longhouse eventually appeared in-between the slim trunks of alders. Sparks flew heavenward from smoke holes, spiralling into a pewter and golden-coloured evening sky. Madelaine steered towards the sea of vehicles that were parked wherever their drivers had decided to stop. She backed into a spot, located her flashlight, and strolled to a covered area that jutted from the longhouse. Here, people were peeling heaps of potatoes and carrots, tossing them into huge pots on Coleman stoves.

A few paces beyond this hive of activity, a group was threading green sticks through the outer edges of one splayed salmon after another. When the threading was complete, each fish was leaned at an angle against a frame of green saplings, over red-hot embers. Madelaine wanted to learn how to thread and tend the salmon.

"Who is it sent you?" asked an elderly man.

She told him about Violet's invitation to attend the celebration, and that she expected she might be asked to help prepare food for the feast.

"You okay with that?"

"Absolutely. Will you teach me how?" She motioned towards the splaying of salmon.

He nodded in the same direction. "Go to him."

Madelaine sharpened tips of green sticks and threaded them through the edges of heart-shaped, silver-backed red and pink gifts from the local ocean waters. She was taught how to lean the salmon on the saplings over the fire, and when to turn them.

"You have done this before?"

"Not with salmon. With skinned rabbit in South Africa."

"No salmon in South Africa, eh?"

"There is a family member of salmon, but they spawn in the ocean. Their life cycle doesn't call them to their home river to spawn like these salmon."

He scratched his chin and grunted a possible assent, which sounded a lot like, "Ah-ho."

At nightfall, Madelaine was guided inside to a room, which was adjacent to the main hall of the longhouse where the feast would occur. Amidst the glow of several hurricane lamps, basins of potatoes and carrots, bags of buttered rolls, and planks of portioned salmon waited to be dished out onto hundreds of plates. Here, a group of women, laughing, talking and chivying young children, welcomed her into the fray. This is where Violet found her.

"You made it! Word from the salmon trench is that you look like a colonial, but your hands work like a BC natural. Good, eh? You hungry?"

"Oh, yes! But shouldn't I wait until everybody is feasting?"

"Nah. There would be no food cooked without us, so we eat now. Serve with a warm heart and a full belly. Help yourself."

She savoured the salmon, having never tasted that fish cooked the way she had now learned; she discovered the smoky flavour exceeded all her expectations of nourishment. As children ate and played, dogs wove in-between legs, devouring dropped morsels, and people joked and jostled, their faces alive with joyful pride. Madelaine was swept into the chatter and laughter until everyone fell silent.

She turned in the direction of their gaze. A warrior had entered their midst. The left side of his face and the right side of his torso were painted black. Another warrior appeared, following him closely. The upper part of his face, from cheekbones up to the hairline, and his muscled belly were painted red. One behind the other, the seven warriors whose songs and dances she had witnessed four weeks ago, painted with unique configurations of red, black, or white, filed past on their way into the throng of people gathered in the main hall.

At Violet's nod, the women began to dish up. Balancing full plates, Madelaine entered the main hall to begin serving, but for a moment, was compelled to stop and greet the sheer power of the energy that had converged under this roof. Momentarily, she was transported back in time to a childhood experience on a farm in South Africa.

Her brother had rescued a barred owl and brought it to the farmhouse wrapped in his sweater. Close to starving and with a broken wing, it was barely alive. They fashioned a splint for its wing and fed it mice caught with the help of the family's Russell terrier. The owl convalesced for a few weeks on the top of her brother's wardrobe.

One evening, they were on a veranda facing the setting sun, preparing to release the owl. Freed from splint and bandage, the owl was perched on her brother's gloved hand, looking towards the horizon. It turned its head to face Madelaine. The deep, fiery glow of the setting sun seemed to have poured into the owl's eyes. Gazing directly into Madelaine's eyes, he transferred that warmth to her.

Oh my! This is like walking into those eyes!

The weight of the plates of food she was carrying brought Madelaine back to the present task. She proceeded into the hall full of people. Back and forth, she and the cooks carried plates loaded with feast food, and returned with empty plates that they stacked on tables, ready to be washed.

Stacking dirty plates a decade ago with a woman whose fingernails were painted the colour of blood, lips caked with scarlet lipstick, hissing, "Smallpox killed them," rinsing her hands in the kitchen sink as if to say, "Get this filth off me": this was an unwanted memory that vanished as quickly as it had risen—one that Madelaine had been carrying like a seed caught between her teeth.

One of the children tapped her on the arm. "Everybody has finished eating. Want to go up top with me?"

"Up top?"

"Come. I'll show you."

The ceremony was soon to begin. Going "up top" meant climbing up on steps notched in the log wall to a crossbeam, then straddling the crossbeam near a plank supporting the roof. Madelaine held onto this plank tightly, summoning the gumption to look down onto the heads and shoulders of people gathered around blazing fires in the centre of the longhouse.

A strong desire to clear the remaining blame she was holding against colonizers took hold of Madelaine when the elders released clouds of eagle down from their uplifted hands, which was instantly borne aloft by the breath of hundreds. Madelaine could now understand how holding on to blame impedes peace and self-respect. Her feelings of shame for loving her mother tongue and those who had taught her fluttered to the rafters where she was perched, dispersing through the smoke hole in the roof. A pleasing weightlessness—the kind that follows one's release from the burden of powerlessness—washed over her and through her.

Final fleeting images surfaced, of that man from Indian Affairs who had sat across the table during Christmas dinner, and his blood-red-nailed and plate-stacking wife; images that now hovered like a charred rag bearing the remnants of his tirade: "Control the savages!" She dismissed the memory that immediately was absorbed into the flames of the ceremonial fire.

Madelaine followed the children's lead to climb down from up top. First, she released her hold on the plank roof support, and then placed both hands on the crossbeam between her knees. Legs dangling, she inched her bum backwards along the crossbeam. Her legs trembled on the climb down the wall, turning to jelly when she reached the floor. She crumpled into a heap right then and there.

Feel so drained. Relieved. Sad.

One of the children dashed off to find Violet and was instantly swallowed by the crowd. Madelaine curled up in a fetal position. People walked by her carefully. Someone placed a cup of water beside her. Madelaine knew that she was safe. She trusted the passers-by and the solid wooden floor beneath her prone body.

I am utterly imbued with satisfaction. Please, someone stop my joy from scattering … lend a helping hand. Just then, a hand brushed her forehead and gently clasped one of hers. She held on to the out-stretched hand like a drowning child, heaving herself to a standing position and into Violet's arms, weeping freely on the kind and supportive shoulder.

"Come," Violet said. "Let's get you home to my place."

During her return trip to Vancouver the following day, Madelaine stood on the deck of the ferry and faced into the force of the wind, knowing that now she had the strength to fly with both wings.

CRANE'S CALL

1980's

The scent of roses greeted Madelaine as she opened the door and stepped into her sister's guest cottage. Fresh and picked at dawn, the blooms were arranged in a glass bowl on the bedside table, next to a tumbler and pitcher of water covered by a circle of beaded netting. It was evening; the curtains, although drawn closed in preparation for the night, allowed the glow of a setting sun to suffuse the room with warm light. A lavender blue counterpane on a single bed, a tartan knee rug folded at the foot of the bed, and pillows in crisp white cotton cases were an irresistible invitation to lie down. A bath would remove the odour of airplane travel—days of it to get from Canada to South Africa—and she probably should be socializing with her sister, brother-in-law, and nieces, but exhaustion had overcome her. Madelaine dropped her luggage in the middle of the room, removed her clothes, and climbed into bed.

Her plan to sleep as long as possible to bridge the ten-hour time difference was foiled by a tumbling collection of memories: her children's voices, and the look in their eyes when she had told them they would be living with their father and his new partner for a while. Madelaine could not bring herself, however, to tell them that their father believed his new partner would become a replacement mother. This off-handed dismissal from her husband's life and that of her children had effectively crushed an already diminished sense of who she was. These circumstances had compelled her to return to her roots in an attempt to reinstate a sense of identity and belonging.

Madelaine must have eventually fallen into an exhausted sleep because when a haunting cry awakened her, it was obvious the night had passed. She sat up to listen, found dawn lighting the room, and came to remembering her whereabouts. More awake now, she heard again what had first sounded like a cry. It was the call of the crowned crane that lived in the garden—the chick her sister had rescued some months before.

Her response to his call was visceral; she felt his yearning and loneliness and wondered how he could thrive on his own, well aware that crowned cranes lived for up to sixty years, and mated for life.

As she passed time at the cottage in the weeks to come, most days Madelaine strolled across lawns and alongside terrace walls where ferns sprouted between stones, sat in the rose garden, and sometimes under the jacaranda tree. She invariably met the crane who also seemed to be strolling in a lonely fashion.

Soon a ritual greeting took shape. She and the crane would come to a standstill about three paces from each other. His fierce amber eyes inspected her bare feet, seemed to skim the outline of her body, and hesitated at her dark curly hair before staring into her blue eyes. His crown of needle-like feathers vibrated and shimmered, the daubs of red on his cheeks turning scarlet as he arched his slender, sinuous neck as if to acknowledge their meeting.

Madelaine looked forward to these encounters and to be sure the crane would find her recognizable, made certain to wear blue jeans and a light-coloured shirt whenever she went strolling. At five and a half feet they were almost the same height, and as they stood eye to eye, she sensed they were absorbing a little of each other.

As recognition deepened he added a new dimension to his greeting. Slowly, as if to give her time to appreciate, he opened his wings and fanned apart the feathers to show cinnamon-coloured fern-like fronds lying between long chalk-white shafts. His open wings, extending to a width of at least seven feet, seemed to be an invitation to walk into the offered embrace. Madelaine had nothing as splendid to show or offer him, which left her mute and still.

Open-winged, dancing intricate steps, even crossing his ankles to make a full body turn, he stretched his neck to its full length, reaching skyward. The sound from his grey feathery breast poured from his open beak, and his call reverberated off the rim of distant treetops. The crane inclined his head as if to listen for an answering call. Hearing nothing, he lowered his head, closed his wings, turned, and strolled away to another part of the garden.

Their daily encounters lasted mere minutes, and yet every time they met, his eloquent courtly dance and the pure symmetry of his body startled her into a clear sense of having exchanged empathy with the lonely existence of another.

Empathy, though, was not something her sister exhibited. She blamed Madelaine for her marriage breakdown, implying that she had always known that marrying at a young age and leaving South Africa would result in disaster, that without close family ties Madelaine was certain to fail, and making it clear her presence disrupted the preferred orderly existence. Already mired in self-recrimination over her failure as a wife and aching for her sons, Madelaine could not bear the further salting of her wounds and expressed this to her sister, who promptly suggested she move to their brother's farm. Madelaine agreed.

On Madelaine's last night at her sister's, the family took her out to a restaurant. Madelaine dressed carefully in black slacks, a pale rose linen blouse, wrapped her head in a fuchsia silk scarf, and put on sparkling earrings. Minutes before they were to leave for the restaurant a heavy rain began to fall, accompanied by a strong wind. The family, already in the car, said they would wait while she fetched her white canvas rain cape from the cottage.

Madelaine ran to the cottage, grabbed her cape, and quickly put it on, securing the clasp at her throat as she opened the door to run to the waiting car. She turned from locking the door and met the crane. He stood there blocking her path, with an expression she had not noticed in previous encounters: keen, almost aggressive, the rain beading and running off his feathered body in tiny rivulets. She darted to one side, thinking she could dash away, but he stepped into her path of escape. A gust of wind caught the left side of her cape, which billowed away from her, flapping like a sail … or maybe a wing? The crane whipped his wings open and began a frenzied dance—not courtly at all.

If I also dance, perhaps he'll remember I am human, not bird, and let me pass by?

Madeleine brandished the cape like a matador's, swirling and whipping it while dancing left and right. She did not like herself for intentionally trying to confuse her friend; she had hoped their farewell would be a sealing of shared respect. This encounter felt fraught with something close to danger. Added to that, the family was waiting and she was drenched from the downpour. She danced until the crane appeared to be confused enough for her to make a run for the car. Settling into the back seat, she simply apologized for the delay and offered no explanation for her tardiness.

Madelaine agreed with her brother's suggestion that rather than staying in the main family household, she move into one of the farm's vacant houses. The one he selected was named "Yonder."

Yonder, built of stone, sat on the rim of a hill about two or so miles from the main house, overlooking a small river meandering across a valley patch-worked into crop fields, paddocks for polo ponies, and pastures for dairy cows.

Simply furnished, the main room and adjoining bedroom were adequate. The kitchen, equipped with basic appliances as well as crockery and cutlery, served its purpose. There was electricity, but no telephone.

The first indications the house had stood empty for some time were the muddy water and worms that spewed from the faucets, the family of field mice living in the kitchen stove warming drawer, and the pair of red-winged starlings nesting on the front porch.

The field mice were so endearing that she did not use the oven. They showed their appreciation by not eating her bread. The red-winged starlings, however, resented her presence and expressed this by dive-bombing her head whenever she went outdoors. A bolt of shock coursed through her body with each whack on the head delivered by a shrieking bird. Hunching her shoulders, protecting her head with both hands, and scurrying out of range of those sharp beaks did little to dispel feelings of banishment. She began to believe they were delivering a daily message that she was unwanted, unworthy, and deserved to be cast out.

Had she, in her compulsion to understand and cope with her own history of being cast aside by her mother and siblings, abandoned her own children? Could her love for her children sustain them while she took time to find clarity? That sadness and hurt she had seen in their eyes dwelled within her, haunting her every attempt to break through the fog of loss.

And now, she had seemingly abandoned the crane, too.

Weeks became months, and the purpose of visiting her siblings to recalibrate herself and secure a firmer footing in life became overlain with survival tasks of a solitary existence in isolation. Madelaine needed a sign to lift her from this present situation—and to provide a sense of direction, perhaps.

The Zulu women working in her brother's house brought vegetables from the garden, fresh bread from the kitchen, and milk and butter from the dairy. She cleaved to their readiness to see to her well being, expressed in the all too familiar tender kindness she had known during childhood. Their visits held her back from the brink of futility. Long walks across surrounding hills and sunlit valleys also kept feelings of emptiness at bay.

One afternoon, while lying on the slope of a hill some distance from Yonder, the haunting call of a crowned crane reached for her.

Searching overhead, she saw a flock of crowned cranes trailing the sky like wisps of smoke, flying toward a field by the river in the valley below Yonder.

She ran, leapt over obstacles in her path, and squeezed through fences, arriving at the riverbank in time to see twenty crowned cranes gathered on a fallow field of dark loam. The sun, low in the western sky cast a glow over the land, rimming their grey bodies in gold. Awed by the solemn purpose these giant birds seemed to be engaged in, she huddled against the trunk of an old, gnarled willow tree at the edge of the field and waited.

The cranes moved about in the field, unhurried, elegant in an atmosphere of gentle peace. Reunions with life partners evoked greetings that began with tender burbling sounds pouring from slightly opened beaks. They caressed cheek to cheek, as if to heighten the colour of scarlet daubs and began calling back and forth. Their voices joined into wave upon wave of jubilant intensity as they began to dance. Sinuous, smoky-grey necks arched, crown feathers shimmered, and opening wings shifted air with a sound like sheets on a clothesline snapping in a breeze. Pairs swooped toward each other; one twirled, and the other bowed and brushed the earth with wing tips. They called in full-throated exuberance, leapt high into arabesques, propelling their bodies to meet chest to chest and then cupping their wings about one another.

All of creation seemed to hold a breath in a world alive with grace as each pair mated in the hushed splendour of a golden evening. Then, in perfect unison, they lifted off from the earth to fly westward into a rose-tinted sky.

An ominous rumble of thunder brought Madelaine back into her crouched body under the willow tree. With no time to mourn the loss of love in her own life, aware of how rapidly storms travelled in this region, and remembering she had left her bedroom window open, she hurried back to Yonder. The wind gathered force and she reached the back door just as heavy rain began to hammer on the tin roof with a deafening clatter. She wrestled the bedroom window closed against a now howling gale and was about to leave the room when, out of the corner of her eye, sensed rather than saw something moving on her bed. There, in the middle of the bed, stood a newborn red-winged starling, wobbling on spindly legs, tiny wings trembling, beak wide open.

The rush of energy that had propelled her through the front door and into the bedroom escaped in a gasp of exhaled breath, instantly replaced by a calm stillness. With utmost care, she placed the fragile bird in the palm of her cupped hand from where it looked at her with fierce, all-seeing eyes. The roar of the storm seemed to suddenly amplify, and yet she distinctly heard a call to surrender emanating from the fledgling.

Rain and wind lashed at the little house. Lightning hissed and crackled. Thunder reverberated off the surrounding hills.

"Surrender."

Yes, that is what she heard. And then she understood that she had a soul debt to settle. With whom, though? Perhaps a way of giving thanks to the Zulu people for raising her with uncondi-tional love? Or maybe she could find work with the tribal people of South Africa? If she earned a salary, her children could come and live with her … .

The storm, having unleashed its fury, moved on. Through a silence intermittently broken by dripping pipes, Madelaine carried the fledgling onto the porch where she reached up with both hands, and gritting her teeth against an imminent attack, placed the baby bird near the nest and slowly backed away. The parent birds glared at her for an instant before tending to their newborn.

Early the next morning, feeling almost brave, she took a cup of coffee outside hoping she would not be disturbed by dive-bombing birds. Nothing happened: no shrieks, and no wings or beaks whacked her head. She sipped coffee in the light of a storm-washed morning, pondering over the tiny bird's message, when a young Zulu boy approached.

First they exchanged greetings, then inquired after each other's health and that of his family, and with that done he handed her a carefully folded scrap of paper, explaining that it was from Madelaine's brother. A reply was expected.

The note informed her of a phone call she was to receive at five o'clock that evening on the farm office phone. Included in the note was an invitation to stay for a sundowner. The young boy carried her verbal reply: she would be there a little before five o'clock.

Her brother was welcoming. Her sister-in-law stayed busy with things not related to the summons. Neither of them were able to tell Madelaine with any certainty who was about to phone. She joined her brother on the veranda and sipped a single malt whiskey while they talked about the weather. The phone rang at five o'clock.

"*Dumela.*[10] I wish to speak with Miss Madelaine, if you please."

"Yes, this is Miss Madelaine speaking."

"Thank you, Miss Madelaine. This here is the Minister of Education in a tribal homeland government. How does the day treat you, Miss Madelaine?"

"Thank you, Sir, the day treats me well." She continued with customary pleasantries, anticipation reverberating through her. "The same for yourself?"

10   hello (Setswana)

"It is well, Miss Madelaine. The reason for my calling you is this: His Excellency, the president, has instructed me to find a qualified educator who will organize and direct the care and learning of our young children. You are to understand that young children are His Excellency's sacred obligation. It is you I am instructed to interview. This is possible, yes?"

"That is possible, Sir. May I ask how it is that you found me?"

He explained that he had contacted a well-known teacher's training institution in South Africa for names of professionals in the field of early childhood education, and that the rector had recommended Madelaine.

"Although," the rector had added, "it's been many years since she graduated, and this woman moves around the world a lot. Her brother would know where she is."

Madelaine accepted the invitation to be interviewed and was on a train travelling north toward the border of Botswana the very next day.

Clackety clack, clackety clack, the train urged as it took her around foothills, over mountains, and across the high plains, the imprint of the fledgling etched into the palm of her hand, and the melody of hope ringing in her ears.

THE MASADI [11]

1980s

❝ Oh, Puna, where *are* they?"

"It is early, my dear. Let us drink our coffee now. Look! The sun. It has not come into our sky yet. Be calm. All will be well. They will come."

Madelaine sips her coffee and ponders all the reasons why she is once again standing in her birth country of South Africa, halfway across the world from her home in Canada. Searching for seemingly impossible work as an early childhood educator for "the blacks" in 1981—in a country governed by racist laws—had fuelled her determination. That, coupled with an undying passion to express gratitude to the tribal people of South Africa and settle a soul debt with the people who raised her played a compelling role in bringing Madelaine to this moment, waiting for women to arrive for the training program she had designed.

11   women (Setswana)

Recollections about the day she had almost given up hope of settling her soul debt, coupled with visions of returning to Canada empty-hearted, paled in comparison to the day when, out of the blue, she was offered the post of Director of Early Childhood Education for a recently established tribal government of the Batswana people. She had accepted.

That was a year ago, during which time she had cemented her commitment to collaborate with South African communities, travelling hundreds of miles to speak with countless people, and receiving valuable guidance about how to best meet the needs of their children. Madelaine's drive to establish a connection with those who were intent on opening an early-learning centre in their region became an obsession.

As if angels were watching over her, she discovered an abandoned mansion, built in the 1800s, on a side street lined with jacaranda trees. Convincing the Department of Education to appropriate the mansion had been a challenge—a battle, one could call it—but relent they did, and the Resource Centre came into being as a training centre and a living accommodation for Madelaine.

She concentrated on resuscitating the neglected orchard and garden at the back, as well as the flowerbeds on either side of the front entrance. Madelaine trained Puna who, with her teaching experience in high schools, had the ability to engage and articulate concepts to groups of learners. This skill and Puna's grasp of the philosophy and practice of working with young children had delighted Madelaine and enlivened their training sessions.

And now, in preparation for the upcoming week, Madelaine and Puna had set up two of the mansion's bedrooms with displays of educational toys and art materials. They stocked the pantry with boxes of tea, cans of coffee, bags of sugar, packets of cookies, matches, and toilet paper.

On this day, they are sitting in the spacious bay-windowed room that had served as the ballroom during the mansion's heyday. Fifty chairs and ten tables arranged in a horseshoe formation face the twenty-foot-long chalkboard. Madelaine is keyed up. She is ready to launch this training program (the first one), but her uncertainty over the lack of response is almost too much to bear. She feels like a river flowing in full spate, approaching a rock wall. With no way forward it will surely burst its banks.

"Not even one reply to all those invitations we mailed! Should I have expected this, Puna? Maybe I did not make myself clear. Could that be why we have not heard from anybody?"

"Ai! *Mosadi*,[12] you worry too much." Puna refills their cups with fresh coffee. "Even if only one person comes today, we will do this training. You will see."

The sun rising over the high desert plains of sub-Saharan Africa fills the room with intense light and casts Puna in silhouette. Her arms extend towards Madelaine with open-fingered hands that dance in the sunbeams, dispelling doubt, infusing hope, and crumbling the rock wall. She places a hand on Madelaine's cheek. Their eyes meet: Puna's luminescent, the colour of root beer; Madelaine's blue and longing to "see" what Puna is so confident about.

"This is only the beginning. You know that, *Mosadi*. For too many generations—so many that we forget—nobody here has said 'yes, African women are important.' We have a saying: 'The man is the head, but we women of Africa know we are the neck.' Ha! *Mosadi*, we can do this thing ... how do you say it ... ? Build a future nation with the children of today."

Raising her arms and turning in a circle, she sings, "We are ready. Great Spirit is ready. Africa's children are ready. And this

12   woman (Setswana)

is ours, *Mosadi*. This place. The garden that is growing out there. All of this is ours. This is where our people will learn new ways for their children."

She stops twirling to take a step towards Madelaine. "And even for those who do not read so well, the pictures you make on the chalkboard … they will help people understand. And me, your Puna, will translate all you say to be sure understanding is going on for everyone. You will see, *Mosadi*. Be patient. Be calm."

As if Puna's burst of confidence has reached into the ether and summoned the *Masadi* from faraway places, footsteps approach the entrance to the Resource Centre. Voices call out, "*nKoko*."[13]

Puna playfully swings her hip against Madelaine, knocking her sideways. She takes her hand. "*Ehe! Aho!* The *Masadi* are here!"

They dance down the passageway together and open the front door.

Women straggle into the Resource Centre in small groups. Puna directs them to Madelaine's office to stow their baggage. Some have come by train. Some hitched rides on trucks, and some have been walking since before dawn. Others rode on donkey carts.

Fortified with tea, coffee, bread, and jam, fifty women settle into the waiting chairs and kick off their shoes. Puna and Madelaine, buoyed by excitement and a good measure of relief, welcome the women and launch the opening day—the first of five.

With Puna translating, Madelaine begins by outlining the concept of the "whole child" and draws a circle on the chalkboard. Within the circle she draws four sections that resemble petals. The petals represent social, intellectual, physical, and emotional development. The space in the centre signifies spiritual development.

13   knock knock (Setswana)

The concept of being whole from the beginning of life is a new idea for many of the women who have, since colonization, been inculcated with the belief that humans are born incomplete and in sin. As the morning progresses, the absorption of the concept is palpable and charged with concentration.

Then this: Madelaine and Puna are explaining the significance of the petals when a strong, melodic voice breaks into song. Madelaine stops with her hand poised to draw on the chalkboard. In unison, like a flock of birds, the women rise to their feet and the room fills with their song. Rich harmony swells to a peak of outpouring. Puna joins them and the room ignites as hands begin clapping a compelling rhythm.

Madelaine feels that her back is pinned to the chalkboard by the sheer force of their voices. Tears trickle into the corners of her mouth, and the piece of chalk falls from her hand. The volume of their song tapers into soft crooning as the women sit down again, ready to resume listening to Madelaine's instruction. Madelaine wipes tears from her cheeks and asks Puna for guidance.

"Go *on, Mosadi*! They are understanding and ready." She retrieves the piece of chalk and hands it to Madelaine. "*Go on*!"

Madelaine's heart is beating wildly. She scans her chalk illustrations and carries on from where they left off before the room erupted with harmony.

At the close of each day, Madelaine's reflections consistently cause her to wonder who is encouraging whom. The influence of these women has altered her teaching methods with the realization that there is more to teaching than sharing transferable skills. Supporting the women and their communities has become a cooperative experience. Walking alongside them opens Madelaine to learn from them while they, quite readily, welcome the knowledge she imparts to them. This, she realizes, is real education. This exchange is transformative for everyone, as education should be.

The fifth and final day of the workshop closes with an awards ceremony, interwoven with whispers of the song that was born on the first day. Puna, inspired by the enthusiastic engagement of the *Masadi*, expresses appreciation by opening her arms to embrace their surroundings.

"Whose is all this, *Masadi*? It is ours! This place is *ours*," she proclaims, and gestures towards Madelaine. "The Great Spirit gave us this woman of light to show us what we can do for our children. We are learning here, in *our* place, how to build a future for our young—how to change things. We *can* do it!"

Each participant receives a certificate of attendance, furthering their mission to find a place within their community where they can set up a centre for young children. Once this has been accomplished, the Resource Centre will contribute art materials and educational toys. The new teacher will receive further training and a government salary.

Amidst farewells to Madelaine and promises to return to the next workshop, Puna escorts them to collect their baggage. Meanwhile, Madelaine prepares a tray of tea and sandwiches for her and Puna to enjoy in the kitchen. They sit down with readiness to assess the workshop and discuss improvements for future ones. Madelaine pours their tea and is about to begin the evaluation, but something is lodged in her mind.

She sets the teapot on the table and pauses. "Puna, before we begin, there's something I need to ask. The *Masadi* … Did they leave through the back door, into the garden?"

"Ai, now you worry again. Yes, that is the way they went."

"But, Puna … why would they do that? The front door leads directly to the street. Y'know, to the trains, trucks, and other transport, no?"

"Eh heh, *Mosadi*, that is so. Maybe they like the garden at the back, nuh?"

Reluctantly, Madelaine forgoes tea and goes to investigate. She discovers the women walking in clusters of pairs, chatting and moving with clear purpose towards the centre of town. Each one is balancing an enormous bundle on their head. Leafy branches tied to the tops of bundles sway and bounce to the rhythm of their steps.

Madelaine kicks off her shoes and breaks into a run. When she catches up with the women at the front of the group she stops and turns around to face them all. With her arms raised high and palms facing them she calls out, "Stop!"

They concertina to a standstill. She takes a deep breath. "*Masadi*, please," and slowly, in English, hoping she will be understood, "I ask you all to return to the back garden. I want to talk to you about something important."

This is what they do, but not without slouching and dragging their feet in sullen silence. Even the branches appear to wilt and sag. Puna is waiting at the gate, a hand on her cheek, mouth agape. Her eyes flicker over each woman as, one by one, they pass along the side of the building, returning to the back garden.

When Madelaine reaches her, Puna whispers, "The pantry—it is ransacked!"

Madelaine needs time to think and calm herself. She enters the Resource Centre through the front door on her way towards the garden, her slow, heavy footsteps resounding on the wooden floor of the wide passageway. She has strived to bring life back to an abandoned garden. The plants and trees have responded beautifully to her nurturing. *How ransacked could the pantry be?* Rage and sorrow threaten to choke Madelaine. She passes the now silent ballroom, their song from the first day a tarnished memory.

The pantry shelves are indeed empty. Madelaine realizes that when she faces the women, her actions must preserve the trust that has been built during the five-day workshop. How can she manage this when she feels so let down—betrayed, even—by fifty women? But then, she has to admit to her naïveté that just five days of training would eradicate the effects of racial marginalization and abject poverty. Madelaine feels foolish.

By the time she reaches the back door, some modicum of dignity has been restored, but it is still uncertain how best to approach the situation without accusing the women of stealing. The fragrance of freshly pulled plants and broken earth greets her as she steps onto the lawn and faces the women. They are standing in a line, balancing bundles on their heads. Behind them, the garden appears ravaged, as if a violent storm has just passed. Resisting any further contemplation and ensuing emotional reaction, Madelaine studies her loyal and remarkable colleague to discern how she is holding up in the face of what has taken place.

Puna is standing as if frozen: arms akimbo, feet planted wide apart, head bent, and face turned away from the women who are staring at her, their faces closed in numb resignation.

Madelaine stretches an arm across Puna's shoulders, hip-checks her, and whispers, "Okay, *Mosadi*. Let's do this now. Ready to translate more new understandings?"

Puna raises her head, eyes Madelaine, and mouths what could be, "How?", or "*Auww!*"

A glint of defeat lurks in Puna's eyes and in the posture of her shoulders, as if the women representing her tribe have revealed a "wound" too dire to contemplate. This observation spurs Madelaine to offer Puna an opportunity to feel empowered.

"Puna, I need your strength and your help right now. Please ask the *Masadi* to lay their bundles at their feet and unpack them."

*Get going*Disgruntled muttering, sharp-eyed resentment, and sighs of defeat disclose their disappointment. The lawn becomes littered with cans of coffee, bars of soap, and rolls of toilet paper. There are boxes of cookies and teabags, bags of sugar, and boxes of matches. Heaps of wilting branches ripped from the fruit trees and vegetable plants torn from the earth, their roots still intact, give the appearance of wilful negligence.

Eyes full of hollow dread, Puna takes Madelaine's hand and whispers, "And now?"

"Stay close and trust."

They face the women; a distant echo of Puna's voice declaring that the building and its contents are "ours" breathes into Madelaine's thoughts.

"*Masadi*," Madelaine begins, "I thank you for coming back so that we may solve this problem together."

And the tandem dance of Madelaine's English and Puna's Setswana once more gets under way, except that it now moves into a realm of "new understandings"—those of personal values.

"Please," Madelaine continues carefully, "be sure in your hearts that I am not thinking of accusation or punishment. I ask you to help me find a way to speak about sharing. Do you remember Puna saying that all of this is ours—our place where we can learn new ways?"

Some women nod. Others grunt their assent.

"This is true. This place *is* ours. But you see, there are many more *Masadi* who will come here to learn. This place is theirs, too. And, you may also return to learn more about working with the children in your communities. So tell me, how can a garden grow if every group of *Masadi* that comes here takes away what is in it?"

The gaze of many shifts to the spoils scattered at their feet.

"Go on, *Mosadi*—go on!" Puna urges.

"If every person who comes to this place takes away soap, matches, tea, and all the government has paid for, how will we be able to ask the government to give us more of these things for future workshops? How can we ask the government to pay you a salary after your learning courses? Who will pay us for taking that which is to be shared with others?"

The woman who had led the song on the opening day steps forward and turns to face the line, throws up her hands, quivering them like a pair of beating wings. "Ai, ai, ai...*Masadi*! The chains of apartheid[14] have given us bad, bad ways—ways that make us believe we are nothing, and therefore *have* nothing. We will not give these ways to our children and grandchildren. We now ask this woman of light to help us because she speaks the truth, *Masadi* ... yes, truth we knew long, long ago."

The woman returns to her bundle on the lawn, Madelaine squeezes Puna's hand, and they then go to each woman to divide her pile of "loot" in half, saying, "*Mosadi*, this half is for you to take home, and this half is for *our* place, where we share with and learn from each other."

A kind of hysteria finds voice in ululation, which reverberates across the wounded garden while the *Masadi* pack their share. With bundles securely tied and deftly placed on each head, the rousing song that pinned Madelaine to the chalkboard five days ago fills the air, dispelling residual tension. United in song, the women saunter onto the street, balancing lighter loads on heads held high.

Hand in hand, Puna and Madelaine listen to the *Masadi* singing until their voices fade beyond earshot. Only then do they collect the remaining items on the lawn and restock the pantry. They will look after the garden tomorrow.

Once seated in front of a fresh pot of tea, Puna heaves a sigh and reaches for her mug. "Yes, dearest *Mosadi*, Great Spirit is good. Do you think He knows that?"

14   apartheid: "apart-ness," the law of racial segregation in South Africa from 1948–1994 (Afrikaans)

A testament to the Masadi's willingness to trust Puna and Madelaine, and the alacrity with which they implemented the skills they developed during the training workshops, became evident between 1981 and 1988. During those years, five hundred early-learning centres for young children were opened. Many flower and vegetable gardens were built. In rural areas, women made mud bricks with which to build centres for their children. In townships, learning centres were set up in vacant buildings.

Puna and Madelaine trained five women to do Madelaine's job in distant regions. By 1986, forty thousand children were experiencing early-learning opportunities. After that first group, Puna and Madelaine eventually trained two thousand women who went on to operate centres within their communities. Each Mosadi received a salary. Madelaine received incalculable love, as well as the freedom to "go on, Mosadi" with a certainty that the process of settling her soul debt was well on its way.

THE THORN SWITCH

1980s

  Go on the road that points to where the sun rises. The land is flat, so you see the line where the sky and earth meet. For a long time you see that. And then on the side of your eating hand there is a line—it is now broken by many, many boxes; hmm … iron boxes—new shining houses. You are not near to the iron boxes when you see them, but look at the side of the road. It is there, at the side of the road—there is a piece of roofing iron with an arrow in paint. It stands up between two stones. Turn your car onto this road. You will travel now to the iron boxes over there."

Madelaine sees the line of the horizon broken by "many, many iron boxes," the piece of corrugated iron between two stones, and the painted arrow. She turns right.

About a week or so before this day, a stoop-shouldered elderly man had come into the Resource Centre asking for "the one who is here for the children." Patting dust from his frayed herringbone suit jacket, he straightened the length of twine holding up his threadbare trousers and accepted Madelaine's offer of tea, sandwich, and chair at her desk.

Smacking his lips after drinking his tea to the last drop, he was ready to explain the reason for his visit. In the area where the government of South Africa had resettled him and many others, "life is going away like sand in the hand." Madelaine must come, he urged, to see the children, to do something for them. She promised she would be there in a few days.

Now, driving slowly over the humps and ruts of the road in her battered old station wagon, she thinks about resettlement camps, the unremitting regularity by which the Nationalist government of South Africa devises increasing restrictions for people of colour.

For example: in the late 1970s, a new law was decreed to "control the blacks," which stated that people from different tribes who were married or living together were doing so illegally. Armed police accompanied by snarling dogs straining at their leashes carried out night raids in order to find and separate those breaking the new law. People's names and tribes were called out. Families were rousted from their beds, prodded with the barrel of a gun, and forced towards one of several trucks, engines idling, and headlights on high beam.

Once every member of a targeted community was accounted for and their tribal origin confirmed, they were loaded onto trucks at gunpoint, and transported to a resettlement camp. Seldom was there time to gather personal belongings. A lasting image many carried in their memory as they were carted away was of their homes burning to the ground, and their loved ones huddled in the back of a truck speeding away to an unknown destination.

Madelaine holds strong views against enforced resettlement, and is of the mind that the Indigenous people of South Africa have undergone pressures and injustices of displacement for far too long, generation after generation, for more than two hundred years.

Row upon row of square, one-room dwellings built of corrugated iron shimmer in fierce mid-morning heat on a barren, treeless landscape. Emaciated dogs, their matted fur crawling with flies, lie in dusty shadows beside dwellings. Cracked plastic basins, odd shoes, broken liquor bottles, and smashed radios litter the sides of the road. Discarded plastic bags snagged on dry weeds festoon empty areas. An air of neglect and hopelessness pervades and threatens to overwhelm Madelaine. She forces herself to stay focused on the children and their needs.

The first thing to do is find the chief, introduce herself, and request his permission to visit the children. She has no idea where his office or home might be. Where can she find someone to provide directions? A grocery store, perhaps. Surely the storekeeper would know where their chief lives.

Where is everybody? There's not a living soul in sight.

Madelaine continues driving, and it is then that she hears the unmistakable voice of Whitney Houston penetrating the desolate silence, singing a song of love. Following the song, Madelaine arrives at a cinder block structure painted bright yellow. Posters glued to exterior walls advertise tobacco and bottled drinks. Madelaine figures she has found the local grocery store.

She approaches the young woman sitting behind the counter. Her hand is drooping over the front of a bulky metal cash register, hanging from an outstretched arm that appears to have been flung there. Her other hand clutches the handle of a radio that sits on the counter. The woman's face, coated with skin-lightening cream, looks like a death mask out of which her eyes stare in hostile boredom. Dusty shelves behind her hold a few cans of beans, packets of tobacco, boxes of laundry soap, and bottles of orange pop.

In response to Madelaine's greeting, the woman jerks her chin. When asked for directions to the chief's house, she nods and with seemingly immense effort raises a forefinger, jabs it away from her, then crooks the finger to her left. By these gestures Madelaine assumes that she is to keep going along the rutted road and turn left somewhere not too far away.

Madelaine drives straight ahead. She comes upon a road on her left, turns, and continues bumping along for a short distance until she arrives at a large cinder-block house with a veranda. A chain-link fence marks the boundary of the property.

She opens a metal gate on screeching hinges, follows a concrete path flanked by used tires partly embedded in the earth, and climbs three steps to a polished, concrete veranda. She knocks on the door.

The sound of a voice from within the house is followed by hurried footsteps. The door opens. Before her stands a strikingly beautiful woman. Her golden brown skin glows. Almond-shaped eyes above high chiselled cheekbones look directly at Madelaine.

"Yes? Can I be of help to you?"

Madelaine introduces herself and explains that she is looking for the chief.

"Yes, I am his wife. Grace. The chief, he is not here. Be certain I will give to him the message of your visit. You may come in?"

Grace indicates the living room, offers a drink of water, and leaves to get the water.

Madelaine glances around the room. There are two armchairs upholstered in brown velvet. One has a leopard skin thrown over its back, which signifies that it is the chief's chair. Two metal folding chairs, each with a small table alongside, cue Madelaine to where she might sit without insulting cultural hierarchy.

She sits on one of the folding chairs facing the armchairs. The polished floor shines, and orange curtains drawn across open windows hang limply. A large oval frame on the wall behind the armchairs holds a black-and-white photograph of a young couple on their wedding day. They stare sombrely into the room, their eyes filled with bewildered hope. The style of their colonial wedding outfits is reminiscent of the 1940s.

Grace returns with two glasses of water, one of which she hands to Madelaine on her way to sit on the second metal chair. As the wife of the chief, Grace's decisions regarding the children of this camp could be crucial to Madelaine's desire to honour the old man's request "to do something for the children."

Grace grants permission for Madelaine to visit the school, and asks how she came to hear about this particular camp. Madelaine speaks about the old man's visit to the Resource Centre, apologizes for not knowing his name, and asks of his whereabouts. Grace tells her that today he is not present. Her curt response indicates an unwillingness to explain further, but leaves Madelaine wondering where he could be.

Madelaine's expressed interest in the wedding portrait, however, unleashes a rush and tumble of words from her hostess— words filled with anguish and pain. Although Madelaine's question might have crossed a social boundary, she senses Grace's willingness to trust her. Therefore, she remains still, eyes lowered, hands folded in her lap, the spectre of forced resettlement held at bay.

Grace eventually releases a deep sigh, seems to harness her words, and sips her water. Her admirable dignity restored, she explains: "That is the mother and father of my husband. They passed on to God in heaven at that time the police and soldiers told us we must move from our forever home of birth."

Her head tilts at a forlorn angle, and her shoulders droop as if deep grief weighs her down. A few moments pass in respectful silence, then Grace rises from her chair, indicating the close of their meeting. She provides Madelaine with directions to the school.

A large shed of glittering corrugated iron casts a broad swathe of shade onto parched earth. Madelaine parks and gets out of the car, listening to a droning female voice and the sounds of children coughing. She searches for windows and an entrance, seeing neither until a footpath leads her to a door-sized sheet of iron, which is attached to the wall of the shed by strips of tires cut to form hinges.

Her knock rattles the sheet of iron. Instantly, sounds from within cease. The door opens and a woman emerges, blinking in the bright sunlight. As she raises one arm to shield her eyes, the door swings away and slams against the exterior wall with a deafening metallic bang. The woman is holding a thorn-covered switch about the length of an adult's forearm.

Madelaine introduces herself, adding that she has the permission of the chief's wife to visit the school. The woman straightens her posture, flicks at the pleats of her skirt, and adjusts her ornate hat—a Sunday-go-to-church kind of hat—before introducing herself as "Miss Teacher Lekubu."

Skin-lightening cream has ravaged Miss Teacher's face. To avoid staring at the oozing blisters on her cheeks and forehead, Madelaine looks into Miss Teacher's eyes, where she meets pools of dark sorrow.

Miss Teacher invites Madelaine into her classroom. Rows of children sit close together on high benches. Their legs dangle above the earth floor. The smallest children, who look to be around three years old, are huddled against each other for support. The other children look to be around seven or eight years old. Madelaine counts forty children.

The air is dense and fetid with the sweat of children trapped in a shed of over-heated iron. A battered desk faces the rows of children. Behind the desk is Miss Teacher's chair—a high-backed, intricately carved chair from an era of formal dining, now held together with baling wire.

Madelaine moves her attention to the thorn switch Miss Teacher continues to hold in a clenched hand, and asks her for it. Miss Teacher whips the switch behind her, clamps her mouth shut, and glares at Madelaine, who wants to glare back. A standoff in these circumstances would defeat the purpose of her visit, however, so instead Madelaine lays out her plan in a firm, quiet voice.

"Miss Teacher, I need your help to get all the children outside and into the shade. In my car, I have oranges, bottles of water, and paper cups for you to distribute to them. But, before we do that, I wish to speak about the thorn switch you hold in your hand. Please give it to me."

Miss Teacher avoids Madelaine's eyes by turning her head to the side, but she hands over the switch. Then she tells the children to line up and marches them outdoors to the shade. Madelaine distributes her supplies to Miss Teacher. While Miss Teacher tends to the children, Madelaine collects crayons and paper from her car and brings them into the classroom.

Fuelled by the need to change whatever she can, Madelaine breaks the thorn switch into tiny pieces and drops them into a garbage bag. She moves the benches to the perimeter of the room and seeks a solution for the heat and revolting smell of sweat. There is a gap in the iron wall where a sheet of iron had come loose. Madelaine props open the sheet of iron with a plank from a broken bench. Fresh air begins to circulate and dispel the suffocating heat and stench. In the cleared space on the bare earth floor she lays out a circle of forty sheets of blank paper, and places a handful of crayons on each one.

She finds Miss Teacher and the children, whom she pictured enjoying oranges and some play in the shade, waiting in line at the door. Madelaine asks her to tell the children to sit on the floor by a piece of paper and draw whatever they would like.

"Ai! *Bato!*"[15] Miss Teacher wails. Her hands clutch at her cheeks. "These children, they do not know drawing. These children have not ever done such a thing. Has Madam come here to see the stupidness?"

"Oh, no, my dear. These children are not stupid, and maybe, just maybe, you will be glad and surprised. Wait and see, please."

Miss Teacher eyes Madelaine with suspicion, but nods to show compliance. She instructs the children to do as asked.

As they shuffle into the classroom their eyes dart around the changed room and alight on the circle of paper and crayons. The line they had been maintaining breaks apart like a snapped string of beads that scatter and come to rest as each child finds a place next to a sheet of paper. Waves of exclamation ripple around the circle. Small hands stroke pieces of paper and move crayons. Giggles erupt and the drawing begins.

Concerned that Miss Teacher may interfere with the process, Madelaine offers her some paper and a handful of crayons while guiding her by the elbow to her desk. Miss Teacher sits down in the chair, lays down a sheet of paper, and begins to draw.

Madelaine leaves her there and moves around the circle to observe children engrossed in making pictures. To sounds of humming, giggles, and excited whispers she moves from child to child brushing her hand across little shoulders bent in concentration, cupping her hands around heads of woolly hair, stepping carefully around feet with calloused soles. With a surge of joy she recognizes what young children all over the world have a natural tendency to draw: stick figures with large heads and huge eyes; round faces with rays exploding outwards; trees, trucks, and

15   expletive (Setswana)

rickety rectangles with windows. The universal language of young children is unfolding right before Madelaine's now misty eyes.

Miss Teacher's drawing is of a bride and groom framed in a repeat pattern of zeroes and crosses.

"Ah, is this your wedding picture?"

Miss Teacher's response is to stare off into the distance as if she is trying to retrieve something.

Indicating the groom, Madelaine asks, "Did he come with you to this place?"

"No, no."

Miss Teacher lowers her eyes to her picture, strokes the figures in it with trembling fingers.

"Oh. So where is he, Miss Teacher?"

"He is of the Sotho tribe. I am of the Batswana. Government, they take him to place for Sotho, many days from here."

"Oh, I am so sorry. My heart hurts with you. Please, come and see the happy surprise your pupils have for you, for me, and most of all, for themselves."

Madelaine takes Miss Teacher by the hand and leads her around the perimeter of the circle of children. The tentative smile on Miss Teacher Lekubu's ravaged face grows wider and warmer. Light now dances in her eyes.

The chief provided land for an early-learning centre. Grace organized women into groups to make mud bricks for the new building and plant a vegetable garden. People from far and near donated a borehole and pump to provide water. The Resource Centre supplied educational toys and art materials.

Madelaine trained Miss Teacher Lekubu and the assistant caregivers. Grace gave birth to a boy during the final phase of the community's project. The early-learning centre was named Utoluthemba ("He Who Finds Hope") after the old man who had come to the Resource Centre. He died a few months after the centre opened.

THE COURT

2005

❝ You, my friend, have to see—well, actually *experience*—this place so that you carry hope for South Africa back to that far north place you call home."

"Sounds good to me, but help me remember, Sue. When was the building of the Court completed? Not that long ago, right?"

"Jah, let's see … it's 2005 now … uh, last year in February, and did you know that it's the first major post-apartheid government structure to be built? I like that the new constitution has its own building. That's a good way to keep the changes safely coming."

Madelaine and Sue have been friends and colleagues for many years. To bring Madelaine's holiday visit with her siblings and their families to a fitting close, her staunch friend is taking her to a place of great significance as a farewell gift.

They drive up Constitution Hill and park on a level area of raw, red-coloured earth at the base of a hill that has recently been dug into and scooped out.

"This parking lot is a recent addition to the Constitutional Court. See the tire tracks left by bulldozers? That's how fresh this is."

"Where were visitors parking before?"

"On side streets. Remember how insane Johannesburg traffic can be? Well, it's worse now, and finding parking spots can make a person crazy! This is much better. C'mon, let's go. It's this way, up those steps. You go first."

The metal steps attached to a steel frame are much like those you see in movies featuring prison life, except that they are leaning against a wall of raw earth and rise from the parking area at a steep ninety-degree angle.

Each footfall on a metal step jars Madelaine's sense of who she is. Her identity, it seems, is unravelling ... *Clang!*

Right now, am I the daughter of colonial Scots and Irish parents who grew up on a farm in South Africa?

Clang!

Am I the girl whose mother tongue is isiZulu?

Clang!

Am I the adventurer who drove from Brazil to Canada?

Clang!

Could the raising of my sons in Canada have shaped me into a North American woman?

Clang!

And what about fleeing the politics of South Africa when the hunt for Nelson Mandela was escalating? Am I still that rebel?

Clang!

Madelaine's next footstep lands on a wide walkway paved with bricks the colour of baked terracotta. Like a carpet runner settling after a vigorous shake, the walkway undulates up a slope for the distance of a city block.

Sue has explained that the new Constitutional Court is built on the site of the Old Fort, a prison built by the British army in the 1800s. Incorporated in the structure of the new Court, materials from the demolished prison, such as the bricks on which she now stands, were recycled. Madelaine recalls that Nelson Mandela was quoted in a Canadian newspaper as saying, " … this Court will stand as a beacon of light, a symbol of hope and celebration, transforming a notorious icon of repression into its opposite. It will ease the memories of suffering inflicted in the dark corners, cells, and corridors of the Old Fort Prison."

She also remembers accounts of the methods of torture inflicted on men and women reduced to "no longer knowing who they are … if they come out alive."

On Madelaine's right, a low windowless building built of large stones and roofed with rusted sheets of corrugated iron assumes the position of a lurker. It exudes such an aura of grief that she imagines hearing sighs and whimpers from decades past.

Ah … that must surely be a leftover of the Old Fort. A searing reminder … .

On her left, a contemporary two-storey building presents with quiet, simple elegance. Its many windows reflect a bright blue sky and white scudding clouds. Attached by rings to each windowsill are rectangles of copper. These appear to breathe as they sway in the warm breeze. Each rectangle reveals engraved laments, eulogies, songs of aching loss and sorrow. Here and there she finds poems blazing with hope and courage.

Mourning Biko,[16]
A star on the floor of this world, raised
Hearts desperate for voice,

16   Steve Biko was a leader of the Black Consciousness Movement in South Africa. Following his arrest he was beaten to death by prison guards in his cell.

Minds acute with desire to overcome.
Astute,
Passionate,
Resonant in courage.
Manacled beaten,
Misunderstood,
Murdered,
Missed.
This blazing star had no hand to hold.
Does he know the embers are not cold?

The embers continue to glow, she whispers to herself and looks at the bricks on which she is standing, on the path aptly named "the Great African Walk."

Sue lays her hand on Madelaine's shoulder. "Go for it! I'll find you later."

This gesture helps Madelaine re-enter the present and continue along the Great African Walk.

Soon she arrives at a dingy, lime-washed building about the size of a two-car garage. Red-coloured earth appears through crumbling plaster like raw sores. Thinking this might be where visitors pay an entrance fee, she steps into a room lit by a single bulb that casts a dim and meagre glow over a drain in the centre of a concrete floor. There are deep gouges in a patch of floor near a hose that is coiled benignly around its drum. At the same instant this bleak scene begins to coalesce in her understanding, she hears human screams of abject terror and pain.

Is the horror I feel in this place asking me something? Do I even have a reply for these writhing ghosts—an apology, perhaps? Can this be real?

Yes, it is real. The screaming sobs are on audiotape. These are the voices of people who were tortured in this very room, and not that long ago.

Madelaine blindly runs for the door hoping to find the Walk, and crashes into a man standing in the doorway. He extends a hand as if to save her from a fall.

"*Hauw!*[17] *Gogo.*[18] I see you. But you are not well? I think maybe you are very not well, *Gogo.*"

Ah, he speaks the language of my childhood—my mother tongue, isiZulu.

Standing before her is a man, slightly taller than she is. His eyes are looking into hers, full of concern. A worried line creases his high forehead on a face that glows like smooth, polished onyx. He places warm hands on her shoulders, and inclines his head towards hers. This instantly calms her trembling arms and legs, and steadies her breathing to near normal. She responds to him in their shared language.

"This is true, son of our nation. I am not well. My heart is bruised and heavy as if a cold stone resides there. This grandmother cannot believe the cruelty, nor understand the minds that inflict life-robbing acts on our sisters and brothers, and on humanity. All my life I have wondered how anyone could believe this is moral and just. I went to live far across the sea to be away from the white man's laws of my place of birth. But then what do I find in the faraway land where I went to live? That unjust cruelty is inflicted on the Indigenous people there also! I cannot lose hope for the liberation of all humanity, but ahh, son of ours …"

He cups the sides of her face with his hands, and wipes tears from her cheeks with his thumbs. She leans into the strength of his fingers and palms cupping her jaw, meeting the intensity shining from his sherry-coloured eyes through the tear-filled blur in hers.

17   oh! (isiZulu)

18   Grandmother (isiZulu)

"*Gogo*, this son of the nation is telling your heart to be calm like washed heaven."

Her eyes clear in time to receive his sky-lighting smile, his open hands gesturing towards the region of her heart. Madelaine watches his hands close as if he has retrieved that which he had reached for. He speaks again. "And now we put that stone out from you, down there with the bricks. Yah! See?"

Madelaine sways with the sensation of having been relieved of a burden. He takes hold of her shoulders and turns her to face the Constitutional Court entrance.

"Go there, *Gogo*, to our Court. That is a good place for you. There you will find *Ubuntu*[19] for your heart."

"*Yebo*,[20] son of our nation, that is what I will now do, and I thank you for easing my heart. *Sala Gahle*."

"*Hamba Gahle*,[21] *Gogo*."

She approaches an exquisite door, thirty feet high and panelled with twenty-seven plaques made from a variety of wood Indigenous to South Africa. Each plaque is carved with symbols and signs conveying the twenty-seven rights enshrined in the Constitution. Many also believe the plaques commemorate the twenty-seven years Nelson Mandela was imprisoned on Robben Island.

Madelaine steps into a spacious foyer. Armchairs covered in earth-toned cloth are arranged in companionable groups on a gleaming black slate floor that appears to quiver as delicate

19   *Ubuntu*: the oneness of humanity (Xhosa)

20   yes (isiZulu)

21   go well (isiZulu)

shadows, cast by the sun shining through crowns of acacia thorn trees, dance and flicker like spots on a moving leopard.

Across the foyer is the entrance to the Court itself—a pair of closed doors panelled with sheets of metals mined in South Africa, a symbol of the wealth denied to the very people who drew them from the earth. To the left of the doors is a larger-than-life photograph of Nelson Mandela beaming his smile of *Ubuntu*; an encouragement to humanity to accept the oneness of us all. That gentle tilt of his head, as if he were listening, instantly takes her back to 1960.

At that time, a meeting or gathering of any kind whatsoever was banned by the Nationalist government. Revolutionaries, freedom fighters, and those who were ready to show solidarity to the anti-apartheid movement were forced to meet in secret locations. It was at such a clandestine meeting that Madelaine met Nelson Mandela. She, speaking isiZulu, had asked him what action she could take to accelerate the fight for freedom. And he, speaking Xhosa, had encouraged her to leave South Africa. "Go, girl!" he had said. "Go out into the world, and stay strong. We will deal with this situation."

Now, holding this memory, she turns to the Court entry doors as they open from within and joins a group of five people who have also been waiting to enter the Court.

Their guide is a broadly built woman dressed in a navy blue skirt and jacket and a white blouse. Wearing her hair in perfectly aligned cornrows, and distinct tribal scarification adorning her cheeks, she invites them to enter.

The group moves forward and comes to a stop at the back row of steeply tiered seats facing a crescent-shaped table—a shape that represents the horns of a buffalo. Eleven high-backed chairs face the tiered seats. The wall behind the table rises to the height of two storeys and is interspersed with balconies to accommodate members of the press. Fanning out to the left and right, walls of rose-coloured bricks end at hip height, at which point they connect with a sweep of clear glass.

Madelaine observes the curve of the walls and the domed ceiling that contains this oval room. She asks the guide about the significance of the curved shape.

"It is the egg of an ostrich, you see. We are inside that egg, where our new constitution was hatched." Her beaming smile as she says the word "hatched" suddenly vanishes. Her voice becomes almost aggressive in tone, perhaps challenging the possibility that these "tourists" may misunderstand her fervour. She places a hand on her hip, juts her jaw forward, and invites everyone to look through the sweep of glass.

"You see the earth out there? You see the trunks of those trees?"

They all turn and bend towards the trunks of the acacias rising from the earth beyond the glass. The guide nods and seems satisfied to have gained their full attention.

"This room. It is like an egg, and it is also like a tree—a tree to shelter our nation. When Africans sit together under a tree, we communicate and discuss problems. We look in here," she pats her chest, "*yebo*, so we can listen and speak about justice and do better for our people. This tree keeps us safe. Safe like truth is safe."

She extends an arm towards the wall and gestures above a section of bricks. Her body language demonstrates great emotion. Both feet are set apart, as if to brace against the anticipated oncoming torrent of familiar grief. She strokes the bricks with her open hand, as one would stroke a fevered brow or a bruised limb.

"See these bricks? There are broken bricks in this wall. You think that maybe we don't know there are broken bricks. We know. They are here to remind us of all the broken hearts; the many, oh-too many broken hearts of our people."

Madelaine curbs an urge to wrap her arms around the woman and simply voices her gratitude. Only as the guide's eyes grow wide and her mouth forms a perfect "O" does Madelaine realize her own outpouring was in her mother tongue.

The guide responds in the same—in isiZulu. "*Hauw*! *Gogo*, you are of us! Your tongue, it has the same root! So, then, you know we can forgive, *Gogo*. You know this takes many, many years to do, but we *can* do it, *yebo*. But forget? We do not forget. We cannot, and we do not forget."

Sue is waiting out front by the entrance doors when Madelaine returns to the sunshine. "Everything awright? You look kinda blown away."

"I *am* blown away, Sue. I need time to reflect, so how about a drink in that place under the trees?"

"A stellar idea, my friend. Let's go."

Following the Great African Walk, Sue and Madelaine return to Sue's car in silence. Madelaine is deep in thought, as is Sue.

The moment Madelaine leaves the brick walkway to descend to the parking area, memories of Zondi, her childhood friend, flood her mind and bring her to a halt on the metal steps.

More than fifty years have passed since their companionable rides through the plantations to and from the village school, their horses' hooves plodding a gentle rhythm, Zondi's lined face the colour of smoked wood, a pattern of scars on his cheeks that identified his tribe, a wispy grey beard, and deep chocolate eyes glowing with kindness … .

Hauw! *Zondi, you visit from beyond the grave? I respectfully greet you, old friend. Yebo, I have not forgotten your words; they remain true in my heart. "nTombi Yethu," you said. "There's no sense in following a path of fear and hatred. Make that a rule for yourself, and never break it."*

About the Author

Helen May was born in South Africa and currently lives in Vancouver, BC, close to her grandchildren and friends. As an avid storyteller, she believes in the power of language to convey life lessons, personal transformation, inspiration, and compassion. She has shared her love for stories extensively throughout her professional life, working as a life story coach, an oral storyteller, and Early Childhood Educator. She continues to facilitate workshops on attaining personal growth through writing and storytelling. Helen is the author of two previously published educational works: *The Possibilities of Music and Stories* (1975) and *It Works* (1987). In *Mother Tongue*, she brings to the page stories she has shared on stages across three continents, offering us a body of emotional and invaluable wisdom about life.

CPSIA information can be obtained
at www.ICGtesting.com
Printed in the USA
LVOW05s1751060416

482218LV00020B/57/P